# Praise for *The Idylwild Cowgirls*

"This is a great story for young girls, focusing on true friendships and the characters' love of adventures on horseback. A young reader can't go wrong riding along in the pages with this group of cowgirls. The story brings back a time when kindness and caring were everyday habits."

> **Shelley F. Mickle**, Author of *American Pharoah: Triple Crown Champion* and *Barbaro: America's Horse*

"Debra Segal, part archivist and part fiction writer, has woven truth and imagination into a nostalgic offering that anyone who knew Paynes Prairie in the '70's will smile at upon reading."

> **Jeri Baldwin**, Publisher and Editor of AgriMag

"Segal's book brings the cowgirls to life along with the times in which they lived. For those who enjoyed Patrick Smith's look at an older Florida in *A Land Remembered,* I recommend putting *The Idylwild Cowgirls* on the same shelf."

> **Barbara Brockman**, Author of *Wound* and six picture books, including *Fantastic Flight*

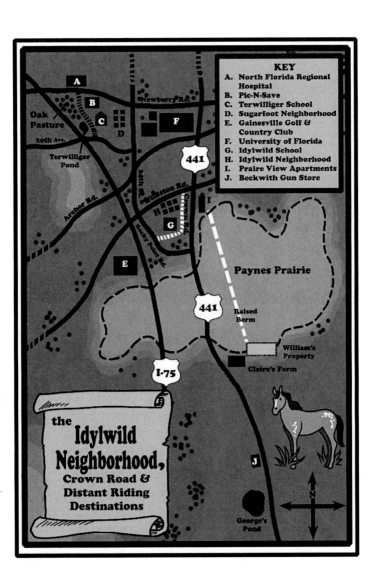

# The Idylwild Cowgirls

Debra Segal

Illustrations by Andre Frattino

Copyright © 2017 by Debra Segal

All rights reserved.

For more information about
*The Idylwild Cowgirls,* visit the author's website
at http://www.IdylwildCowgirls.com

Printed and bound by Alta Systems, Inc.
Gainesville, FL
Fourth Printing


ISBN: 978-164007339-5 (paperback)
ISBN: 978-164007340-1 (e-book)

## *Gainesville, Florida, 1973*

## Chapter 1

Jodi pedaled hard, with a purpose, dodging the potholes in the dirt road. She pumped the right pedal, then the left, in rapid succession as her body swayed from side to side with the metal frame. She was gaining, but she couldn't catch up before the riders vanished around the next curve. Harder she thrust the pedals, commanding all the pedal power that her 13-year-old legs would give.

"Ouch!" she cried out. Her front wheel struck a hole and her knee slammed into the base of the handlebars. "Whoa!" she yelled as her bike began to oscillate back and forth.

Jodi struggled to regain control but another pothole dumped her onto the dirt road. Shaken, she laid there a moment. Then she painfully lifted herself and her bike out of the road, remounted, and continued her pursuit.

When she rounded the corner, the two equestrians were half a block away. Harder she cycled, refusing to give up, and ignoring the sweaty strands of hair that partially blocked her view and the pains in her body that screamed at her to stop.

"Hey there!" Jodi called out when she was within shouting distance of the two riders.

The pair reined in their horses and turned to see a scuffed-up girl with a torn wicker basket approaching.

Jodi braked by the riders. She gazed up at the two equestrians – a tall girl on an Appaloosa and a bespectacled girl on a pinto - and then quickly diverted her eyes as she flustered over her disheveled appearance and tattered bicycle. An awkward silence ensued, interrupted only by Jodi's loud breathing and the Appaloosa stomping its foot in protest of a pesky fly.

Finally, the rider on the spotted horse cleared her throat. "You musta ridden hard to catch up with us."

Jodi nodded as she gasped for air. She looked up at the tall girl on the enormous horse. The pair's combined height rivaled the tallest bushes that lined the dirt road. Being the progeny of short parents, Jodi was oblivious to her small stature. But now she felt like an ant, albeit a scraped up and sore one, next to a giraffe.

The girl on the brown and white pony nudged up her glasses and squinted at Jodi. "What happened to you? Your arm's bleeding and there's dirt on your face. Did you wreck on your bike?"

"Yeah," Jodi mumbled as she instinctively brushed off some sand. But the sweat that streamed down her face caused the grit to adhere to her cheek.

The giant straightened her shoulders. "My name's Andi. What's yours?" Andi sat tall on her Appaloosa. Her straight blond hair, bleached by the sun, covered her shoulders and part of her faded t-shirt. Her bell bottom jeans barely concealed her shins, exposing her ankles, bare feet, and drawing attention to her unusual height.

"My, my name's Jodi," she stuttered as she shifted her eyes upward to the oversized girl with the commanding voice. "I, I just moved here and I've wanted a horse ever since uh, uh, since forever."

## Chapter 1

Andi nodded. "That's Kris," she said as she gestured to her companion who was straddling the pinto.

Kris nudged up her glasses and smiled. "Howdy, Jodi. Welcome to the Idylwild neighborhood."

Dressed in shorts and a well-worn yellow t-shirt, Kris was slender, tan, and completely at ease on her pony. A pair of wire-rimmed glasses rested on her nose, and a faded blue bandana constrained both her brown hair and the temples of her glasses. Jodi reckoned that Kris was 13 years old like she was, or 14 at most. Jodi admired Kris's brown and white pony with its long, shiny mane and smooth, satiny coat. She thought longingly that if I ever get a horse, no, *when* I get a horse, I will brush it for hours until its mane and tail and entire body sparkles like that.

Jodi was jolted back to the conversation by Andi's powerful voice. "If you want a horse then you sure moved to the right neighborhood. There's plenty of places 'round here to ride to. And we know all the trails 'cause we've been riding 'em for years."

"Yep," Kris agreed, "This here dirt road is called Crown Road on account of the Crown family who lived here a long time ago. It's mine and Patches' favorite place to ride." She reached down and stroked her pony's neck, which caused her cumbersome glasses to slip down her nose.

Andi swept her hand grandly. "Sometimes we ride all the way across Gainesville to Terwilliger Pond so we can swim with our horses."

"We even ride out past Paynes Prairie. Out that-a-way," Kris gestured.

"Hop on Bingo and we'll show you the neighborhood," Andi said in her take-charge voice. "He won't mind two people ridin' him. Shoot, he probably won't even notice, given how uh, small you are."

Jodi didn't expect the invitation to ride, but she wasn't about to let her shyness interfere. She started to drop her bike right in the middle of the dirt road when Andi intervened.

"You can leave your bike at my house. It's just around the corner. Follow us."

Jodi peddled close behind, entranced by the riders and their lovely horses. She watched the two equestrians – tall, strapping Andi and petite Kris - as they flowed effortlessly with every stride their horses took. Their horses were just as different as the riders. Andi's mount was the Great Dane equivalent to Kris' sleek little Beagle. The two horses not only contrasted in size but also in their markings. Bingo, the Appaloosa, wore a chocolate-colored coat that popped with white and tan spots. Patches' small frame was draped with bronze and ivory, and her thick tail threatened to drag the ground. Bingo's tail looked like an after-thought, a sparse collection of hairs that barely reached his hocks. But layered on both sides of his stub-of-a-tail were big powerful muscles, strong enough, Jodi thought, to haul a cart full of people straight up a mountain.

They entered Andi's side yard from a path. Jodi leaned her bike against a tree and stared up at Andi who was perched on the enormous horse.

Kris shook her head. "Hey girl, just climb up the boards on the fence and jump onto the horse."

Andi navigated Bingo over to her passenger. "Grab my hand and swing your right leg over."

In one nervous moment Jodi was sitting behind the giant on the tallest horse she could ever have imagined.

The trio headed back to Crown Road. At first, Jodi held her body rigid, unsure of the gelding's big, powerful gait. But she watched how at ease the other two riders were, and soon relaxed and let her legs dangle and her hips move back and forth in

## Chapter 1

rhythm to the horse's stride. Jodi gazed up at the gigantic oak trees and the massive branches that shielded the road and the riders from the hot, glaring sun. Robes of moss drooped from the trees' outstretched arms. A car approached and the equestrians reined their horses to the edge of the road and halted while the vehicle slowly drove past. The girls smiled and waved to the driver.

"Wow," Jodi exclaimed. "I wondered what you did when a car passes by."

"Folks round here drive slow on Crown Road, and they've always been real nice to us horseback riders," Kris explained.

"All the neighborhood folks, all except Mr. Moody, love Crown Road. It's our Equine Highway," Andi proclaimed proudly. "My dad says there's no other road in all of Gainesville that's as beautiful as this road."

Jodi was puzzled. "Why doesn't Mr. Moody like Crown Road?"

Kris's expression switched to one of grave seriousness. "Because he wants to build a bunch of houses on his land. If he can get the county to widen and pave the road, then he can sell his property to a developer and get rich."

Jodi gasped, "Oh no, they would cut down these beautiful trees and destroy your riding road."

"That's right," Andi nodded, "But we'll fight Mr. Moody and the county too if they mess with our road."

The three continued their stroll down the dirt road, shaded by the majestic century-old live oaks. So in-the-moment were the three teenage girls that they didn't notice the scolding Carolina wren hiding in the nearby wax myrtle thicket, or the high-pitched "*keeyuur keeyuur*" of the red-shouldered hawk as it circled overhead. This raptor was particularly vocal since it had recently fledged its nest and was still learning to master its big, powerful wings.

"Hey," Kris exclaimed, "I'm thirsty. Let's ride over to the school and get some water."

"Good idea," Andi replied.

The two girls reined their horses right and veered onto a side trail through a forest of oaks, sweet gums, and cabbage palms. They navigated single-file along the narrow path, occasionally leaning left or right to avoid a branch or a big spider web and its resident spider.

"Do you ever gallop along here?" Jodi asked from her backseat position.

"Yep," Andi answered. "But we have to be careful of the boys on motorbikes 'cause they will try and spook our horses."

"Why would they do that?" Jodi asked.

Kris laughed. "Cause me and my sister tricked 'em into tryin' to ride Patches, but Patches wasn't broke yet, so she bucked one of 'em off. Ever since then, those boys have been real mean to us."

"We'll have plenty of warning before they show up," Andi explained, "since their motorbikes are so noisy."

Jodi was awed at the beauty around her and the feel of the horse transporting her through her new neighborhood. They soon reached their destination - Idylwild Elementary School - the neighborhood grade school that administered lessons on reading and arithmetic to all the neighborhood kids.

Kris pointed ahead. "The water fountain's over there."

They steered their horses down the sidewalk until they reached the fountain that protruded from the side of the school's red brick wall. Kris slid off her pony, readjusted her glasses, pressed the shiny button, and drank from the stream of water.

*Chapter 1*

Then she turned to her pony. "It's your turn, little girl. Do you want some water?" Patches cocked up her ears, stretched out her neck, and began to slurp.

Andi navigated her horse to a concrete bench so Jodi could slide down. "Does Bingo drink water from the fountain too?" Jodi asked.

"Yep, 'cause he knows it might be a couple of hours before he gets another chance for water."

As Jodi drank, she savored the lingering aroma of horses, sweaty horses, a scent she hoped would continue to enrich her summer days.

Andi and Kris led their mounts to a patch of grass under a tall pine tree. Jodi followed in silence as she thought of questions to ask the girls. She wanted to know all about their horses, if there were others with horses in the neighborhood, and if they rode every day during the summer while school was out. She asked many of those questions but wasn't entirely focused on the answers as she was mesmerized by the two lovely animals that towered over her as they grazed contently.

After a spell, the horses jerked up their heads and cocked both ears forward. A few seconds later, a towheaded girl riding a large palomino emerged from the trail.

"Howdy, Tessa!" Andi and Kris called out as they waved.

Tessa guided her palomino effortlessly over to the group. "I was hopin' to find y'all here."

Andi took charge of the introductions. "This is Jodi. She just moved here, and she wants a horse."

Jodi wanted to interject in capital letters, REALLY wants a horse, but she just waved shyly and said, "Hi."

Jodi noticed that Tessa was small too, just like she was. Blond curls dangled to her shoulders. Her cheeks were fired pink by the summer sun, which partially concealed the freckles that peppered her round face. Like the other riders, Tessa was completely at ease on her tall horse.

Tessa greeted the newest neighborhood resident. "You sure moved to the right place 'cause almost all of us have a horse." Tessa switched to a serious tone as she addressed the group. "You won't believe what just happened to me! As we trotted over here on the trail, we overshot one of the curves." Tessa's

## Chapter 1

eyes widened and her voice rose. "As I guided Speedy back to the trail, the ground began collapsing!"

"What do you mean *collapsing*?" Andi asked.

"A hole opened up and dirt started disappearing underground. Speedy's back leg got sucked into the hole and he fell down onto one knee."

Kris was alarmed by Tessa's story. "What did you do?"

"I kicked Speedy hard and yelled at him to keep goin'. He lunged forward and finally caught his balance."

"That's scary!" Andi exclaimed.

"No kiddin'! I watched more dirt and then a small tree get sucked into the hole. Then the hole filled with sand and it all stopped."

"Sounds like a sinkhole opened up. Let's ride over and see," Kris suggested.

"OK," Tessa replied. "But I need some water first."

Jodi studied the horse that was transporting Tessa. The palomino was almost as tall as Bingo, but not nearly as powerful looking. His coat was a soft cream color, and his mane and tail were silky white. His large dark eyes suggested a calm, kind, and sensible demeanor. Perhaps, Jodi thought, the best disposition to have in the face of danger, like a sinkhole opening and threatening to swallow both horse and rider.

The group retraced their steps along the trail, and when they reached the spot, Tessa pointed to a sandy depression. "That's it! Don't go any closer!" The ground didn't appear threatening, but the indentation of exposed sand tagged it as quite different from the surrounding woods.

Kris broke the silence. "Look, there's the tree that was almost sucked into the ground. It's leaning sideways, and half its trunk is buried."

"Tessa, get your daddy to rope off the area so no one else rides over it," Andi demanded.

"Good idea," Tessa agreed. "Come on, let's ride to my house and see if my daddy's home." As they rode single file along the trail, Tessa called back to Jodi. "Are your parents gonna get you a horse?"

Jodi wanted to shout, "YES!", but she responded more hesitantly. "I really want one, and my momma thinks I should have one, but my daddy says he's too busy to build a fence around our back yard. I would start building it tomorrow if I knew how. I know I'm small, but I'm already 13, and I'm stronger than I look. If we had a fence around our back yard, I just know my daddy would buy me a horse."

The group remained mute for a long moment, long enough that Jodi worried she might have said something wrong.

Then Tessa broke the silence. "My daddy's a carpenter and he's good at buildin' things. He built my horse fence. I'll ask him if he'll help you build a fence in your back yard."

"If Tessa's dad will help you, then we'll all help you build the fence," Andi announced decisively. "We've repaired fences, dug post holes, and nailed up boards. We can all help."

Jodi beamed with excitement. "You mean all of the Idylwild Cowgirls will help me and Tessa's daddy build my fence?"

"*Idylwild Cowgirls?*" Andi considered as she exaggerated the two words. "We've never been called that before."

"Well, we idle around on our horses," Tessa replied.

"And we sure are wild," Andi laughed.

"Especially you," Kris said as she pointed at her long-time friend.

*Chapter 1*

"So now we're the Idylwild Cowgirls," Andi proclaimed proudly as she towered over the other riders. "And yes, all of us Idylwild Cowgirls will help you build your fence."

At that moment, Jodi realized her dream of owning a horse had just galloped a giant stride closer to reality.

## Chapter 2

A plan was developing, one that was such a long shot that Jodi wondered if she really would get a horse. But school was out for the next three months and she was determined to execute her plan.

As the girls agreed, Tessa would ask her dad if he would help build a fence around Jodi's back yard. Jodi would ask her dad, or beg and plead if necessary, to buy the fence-building supplies. Andi and Kris would solicit support from the other cowgirls. This would be a neighborhood fence-raising project, that was of course, if both dads agreed.

The next morning, Jodi aimed straight for Andi's house, cranking hard on the pedals but more cautiously avoiding the potholes along Crown Road. She entered the side yard just as Kris was arriving on her pinto. Several minutes later, a young girl trotted up on a chestnut-colored horse, her face flushed scarlet and her unruly brown curls bouncing in all directions.

"I told you to wait for me!" the youngster screeched as she tugged on the leather reins. Her horse objected to the roughness and shook its head from side to side.

Kris shot her an angry scowl. "You take too long to get ready, and besides, you know how to get here." Kris turned her attention to Jodi who was still straddling her bike. "That's my little sister, LeeAnne."

*Chapter 2*

"Hi," LeeAnne said as she pushed back the ringlets that partially covered her eyes. "You don't mind if me and Daisy come awong, do ya?"

"No, of course not," Jodi said, hoping she wasn't interfering in the sisters' rivalry.

LeeAnne was young, probably only seven or eight-years-old, and to Jodi, she seemed hardly old enough to ride alone. LeeAnne wore a dingy blue T-shirt, well-worn bellbottom jeans, and old tennis shoes. The bareback pad that hugged her mount's narrow sides was sun-faded, and strips of foam poked out of several holes. Jodi wondered if LeeAnne was the recipient of this hand-me-down piece of tack and if her older sister had traveled the many miles in it before relinquishing it to her younger sibling.

They found Bingo tied to a corner post while Andi brushed his spotted coat. Forgetting to say hello, Jodi blurted out, "I can't wait to find out if Tessa's dad agreed to help me build my fence."

"He's a real nice man," Andi nodded. "He probably will."

Andi carefully slid the bit into the gelding's mouth, lifted the leather headstall over his ears, and tossed the reins onto the horse's neck. She gripped a wad of mane with her left hand, crouched slightly, and swung her right leg up and over Bingo's back. Jodi climbed up the board fence and stepped onto Andi's outstretched foot while Andi hoisted her onto the back of the long-legged Appaloosa. Kris led the way to Tessa's house, followed by the two girls in tandem. LeeAnne trailed close behind. They were off to see Tessa's dad for a most important conversation.

As the group ambled along Crown Road, Jodi again admired the majestic oaks and the massive limbs that provided a shady canopy over the dirt road. This time she noticed wildflowers in the fields and resurrection ferns covering many of the large branches. She had learned from her mom, an accomplished gardener, that with rain, resurrection ferns will transform almost instantly from a mass of dried-up fronds to a carpet of green ferns. The rain that fell last night had triggered the resurgence of the aerial plants.

LeeAnne trotted her horse up until she was striding next to the two tandem girls. "Have you widden a hohse vewy much?" she asked Jodi as she flicked at some curls that insisted on blocking her view.

"Yeah, a few times at my cousin's farm," Jodi answered.

"It's not vewy hawd. You just gwip with your wegs and hold on," LeeAnne replied.

Jodi noticed that Daisy, LeeAnne's horse, was not as sleek or healthy looking as her sister's mount. The mare was thin and her coat a dull chestnut color.

Tessa was waiting for them when they arrived. She waved and gestured for Jodi to slide off Bingo and follow her to the building near the house. Jodi heard the deafening sounds of a table saw as she entered the workshop. Tessa gestured to the man running the saw and pointed at Jodi. The man nodded, turned off the screaming machine, and lifted the safety glasses that partially covered his tanned face. Jodi noticed the blond hair that outlined his blue baseball cap, the same golden hair color as his daughter's.

Tessa approached the smiling man and shouted so she could be heard over the machine that was gradually screeching to a halt. "Daddy, this is Jodi, the new girl I told you about last night."

"Well howdy, young lady," he drawled. "So, ya wanna horse, do ya?"

## Chapter 2

"Oh yes," Jodi answered. "I've always wanted a horse. We have plenty of room at our new house, but my daddy doesn't have time to build a fence in our back yard. I would do all the work myself if I knew how."

The carpenter nodded toward his daughter. "My youngin' here asked me if I would help you and your dad build a fence. But I can't say yes or no without meetin' your dad and talkin' to him."

Jodi blurted out nervously. "Last night I told my daddy you might help us and he said he would be mighty pleased to talk to you, sir. Could you come over tonight and meet him? He'll be home by 5:30."

Mr. Brown nodded. "Tell me where you live, young lady, and Tessa and I'll drive Old Jezebel over there this evenin'."

Tessa noticed Jodi's confusion. "Old Jezebel's my daddy's antique car that he rebuilt. He likes to tinker with old cars as much as I like to ride horses."

Mr. Brown's face warmed at the reference to his hobby. "Yep, old Jezebel ain't a hay burner and she don't need a fence." Winking, he added, "She's a whole lot easier to keep than those horses of yours."

Tessa hugged her dad, kissed his cheek, and turned to Jodi. "Come on, let's catch the horses. I'll ride Speedy and you can ride my pony, Snuffy."

The girls departed down Tessa's driveway and onto Crown Road. Jodi couldn't believe her eyes, or her legs that were wrapped around the narrow barrel of a chestnut pony. She reached down and petted Snuffy's soft furry neck, and the pony cocked his left ear back toward his new rider as he kept pace with the long strides of the horses ahead.

*The Idylwild Cowgirls*

As 5:30 approached, Jodi could barely contain herself. Tessa's dad would soon arrive to discuss the fence-building project for the horse she hoped her parents would buy her. Jodi reflected on the discussion she'd had last night with her parents and the shocked look on their faces when she told them she found a professional carpenter to help her build a fence around the back yard. She just needed her dad to buy the supplies, and then Jodi and the carpenter and her new friends, the Idylwild Cowgirls, would do the rest.

Jodi and her dad were in the back yard searching for the short metal stakes that marked the corners of their newly purchased property when they heard a deep, resonating sound. They hurried to the front yard and found Mr. Brown steering a bright red Chevy Bel Air into the driveway. Tessa sat in the front seat of the convertible next to her father and waved when she spotted Jodi and her dad.

The two men introduced themselves and Mr. Brown initiated the conversation in his deep southern drawl. "Your daughter tells me she wants a horse, but y'all need some help with the fence buildin' part."

"Is that so?" Mr. Robertson replied.

Mr. Brown motioned to the back yard. "Let's take a look at your yard."

The two girls listened as the men discussed the many aspects of building a fence – where the property corners were located, the best type of wire to use, the distance between fence posts, and where the gate should be located.

Mr. Brown shoved his hands into his blue jeans and cleared his throat. "I don't mind helping y'all build a fence. Lord knows I've built a few miles of fences between the ones on our little farm and the ones for my customers. And I'll tell you what I discovered with my little gal. I bought her a horse, and then I

## Chapter 2

quit worrin' about her grades, her gettin' lazy, or her gettin' into trouble. We have one simple rule at our house. Do good in school, shoulder all the responsibility, and don't get into no trouble, then you can keep ridin' your horse. Mess up, and that horse don't get ridden for a long time."

As the men talked, the girls spotted some movement down the dirt road and recognized the three riders – Andi, Kris, and LeeAnne - cantering toward the house.

"We all want to help build your fence!" Andi called out as she reined her horse to a stop.

"Yeah," Kris added. "We're all here to help you."

Mr. Robertson looked around at the army of workers that his daughter had assembled. "Ok, ok, give me a week to buy all the materials and then we can start."

## Chapter 3

During the week, Jodi and her dad planned the fence-building project. They laid out the footprint of the fence using cinder blocks and rope. Next, Jodi marked the approximate location of the fence posts using pine cones and sticks. They determined they would need four corner posts, two additional thick posts to hang and support the gate, and 110 fence posts.

"Wow!" Jodi exclaimed as she gazed out at the skeleton of the fence she and her dad had laid out over the past several evenings. "This pasture will be plenty big enough for a horse."

By the end of the week, Mr. Robertson had purchased a huge pile of fence posts, a post hole digger, fence wire, fence staples, a gate, and other fence-building tools. Jodi was so anxious to start on the fence that she ran out back with the new post hole diggers and tried to dig a hole at the first marker she encountered.

"Whoa there, sport," her dad called out. "Those holes will probably shift after we install the corner posts and stretch out the wire."

Fence-building activities began in earnest the next day. Right after breakfast, Jodi and her dad prepared for the new construction project. Even Jodi's younger brother, Sam, who had shown no interest in the impending horse project, asked to join in. Jodi figured that the prospect of meeting her new friends was the carrot that enticed Sam to participate. And she knew

## Chapter 3

that lots more carrots would be doled out when she finally got her own horse.

A low rumbling sound announced the arrival of Tessa and her dad. After the two men greeted each other, Mr. Brown announced, "I brought over another post hole digger and a come-along so we can stretch the wire tight before we hammer the staples."

The cowgirls arrived on their bicycles. First Andi, followed soon afterward by sisters Kris and LeeAnne. Jodi introduced them to Sam who waved shyly and then attempted to divert their attention away from him by looking down and brushing some imaginary dirt from his pants. Kris and LeeAnne brought work gloves, and Andi announced that her mom would deliver a platter of egg salad sandwiches at lunch time.

The four older girls carried fence posts to the marked intervals while the two younger kids – LeeAnne and Sam – watched more than they assisted. The men installed the first two corner posts, a task that was complicated by the need to brace the massive poles in opposite directions.

"Now we can stretch a bottom wire between these two corner posts, so we hava straight line for this row of posts," Mr. Brown drawled. "Then the girls can dig the holes for this side of the fence."

Andi laughed as Jodi gripped the post hole diggers. "You ain't nearly as tall as them handles. How do you suppose you're gonna dig a hole with em?"

Jodi was determined to help build her fence. She imitated the men's technique as she lifted the two wooden handles and shoved the metal jaws into the ground. But the jagged bucket barely pierced the carpet of grass. Jodi opened the two handles, a motion that caused the auger to grasp the sod, and then lifted the tool up. To her dismay, the metal bucket was empty.

Mr. Brown saw Jodi struggle and called out as he walked over to her. "Hey there, young lady, let me break through the grass and get the hole started for ya. That should make it easier," he winked.

The girls alternated digging holes along the stretched-out wire that defined the north side of the new fence. Andi, the tallest and strongest cowgirl, often started the holes and then switched off to one of the others to finish. After digging through

## Chapter 3

the thick sod of one of the holes, Andi turned to Kris and joked. "This hole's ready for your skinny arms to finish."

Kris glanced at her lanky but tan arms and then shot Andi a fake scowl. "Thanks a lot." Kris didn't take her long-time friend's comment personally. She knew it was just typical, fun-loving, jokester, Andi.

As lunch time approached, the girls had only installed six posts along one side of the fence. The bottleneck, it seemed, was that there were over 100 holes to dig, but only two augers. And the men were using one of the tools to install the corner posts.

"If only we had another post hole digger," Jodi said, "then three people could dig holes at the same time."

"I'll call my mom and ask her to bring ours over when she brings the sandwiches," Andi offered.

The girls dug holes all afternoon, mining out the soil horizons one auger bucket at a time. The day ended with all four corner posts and 15 smaller posts standing vertically with their bases tightly packed into the earth. Nine posts remained to be installed along the first side of the fence. The cowgirls stood weary, shoulders slumped, and dirt streaked across their clothes and skin.

Mr. Brown reassured the exhausted workers. "We accomplished much more today than it appears. It takes a whole lotta time to install and brace those big heavy corner posts and carry and lay out all them other posts. Why look at all the holes y'all dug and the posts you put in. You'll see," he nodded, "the rest of the fence will go up much faster than today."

They all agreed to meet the following Saturday to continue building the fence. As Mr. Brown opened the door to his antique Chevy, Mr. Robertson turned to him and said, "I don't know how to thank you for all your help today. I'm still amazed you would spend all this time and effort to help a complete stranger build a fence."

Mr. Brown smiled. "You and your sweet, determined daughter ain't strangers no more." He paused a moment as he looked over at his worn-out daughter collapsed in the seat across from him. "You know, there's a special bond between gals and their horses. Now Jodi's gonna have the same opportunity as these other lucky ones."

# Chapter 4

Claire lived on a farm several miles south of the Idylwild neighborhood. She and Tessa were friends from school, but she didn't know any of the other cowgirls. Claire hoped to eventually ride her horse to the Idylwild neighborhood so she could ride with Tessa and meet the cowgirls. But her new horse was too young and inexperienced for the long commute.

Shotsie, Claire's new horse, was a flashy 3-year-old chestnut with four white stockings and a blaze that stretched from jaw to jaw. Claire began weekly riding lessons so she could learn how to properly train the young gelding. During the lessons, Claire was taught how to convey subtle and consistent cues, while resisting strong hand movements.

"Remember, your hands connect directly to the horse's sensitive mouth through the reins," her instructor had explained. "Rough hands make for a resistant horse."

Claire rode her new horse almost every day, but she heeded her instructor's advice - start out slow, reward him frequently with kind words and gentle pats, and be sensitive with your cues. As the pair progressed, Claire gradually rode for longer periods and further distances. She introduced him to distractions and obstacles because she wanted him to be bomb-proof and to trust her, especially in new and strange surroundings. She schooled him near her dad's cows, slowly weaving in and out of the grazing herd. She trotted next to the tractor as her brother mowed the pastures. She even nudged him into the garage and told him to stay while she ran inside and retrieved a carrot, his reward for obeying a more typical canine command. She taught him to walk through the creek that flowed across the farm. Once he acquiesced, she trotted through the waterway. When that feat was accomplished, she cantered across the meandering stream, sending spray in every direction. Claire marveled at how willing and brave Shotsie was. Together, they were learning to communicate and trust each other.

One morning, Claire rode back to the forested area at the far east end of the farm. As she walked along the perimeter path, she heard a chorus of sounds radiating from the woods. Claire briefly wondered what types of birds created such animated songs when a female cardinal with a large insect clutched in its bill caught her attention. She halted her mount and silently watched as the eye-level parent hopped from limb to branch and then slipped into a woven nest with its gift for the hidden infants.

Shotsie was also alert to the sounds of the woods. As the pair continued along the trail, he alternated between cocking both ears forward and shifting one ear back in anticipation of a signal from his rider. Claire cued her mount to trot and the chestnut shifted to an energetic, trail-blazing stride. They jogged along the entire north perimeter, rounded the corner, and continued their cadence along the eastern fence line.

Then, without a signal from his rider, Shotsie halted abruptly. Standing up ahead in the trail was a deer with big, brown ears that were fully alert to the approaching horse and rider. The two mammals stared at each other while Claire averted her stare in hopes that she would not be perceived as a predator and cause the wild animal to bolt. She sat still in the

## Chapter 4

saddle, slowing her breathing and not moving a muscle. With eyes transfixed, the doe walked cautiously toward the horse. And without a nudge from the rider, Shotsie stepped closer to the deer. The two creatures continued their slow, tentative advance while Claire remained rigid in the saddle, trying not to disrupt this chance encounter.

As the doe approached, Claire noticed the similarities as well as the striking differences between the two animals. The deer was much smaller and thinner than her tall horse. Its tawny brown coat was coarse and flecked with white highlights. Its ears were proportionately larger, the most prominent feature on its triangular face. Its round, youthful eyes expressed a sense of curiosity that overrode caution.

The deer twitched its back nervously as it advanced toward the pair. When a mere arm's length separated the two ungulates, they extended their necks and touched noses. Then the doe retreated a step, glanced up at the motionless rider, turned, and with her white tail raised like a flag, high-stepped through the woods. Claire and her horse remained spell-bound for a long moment before they continued their trail ride.

# Chapter 5

By early summer, several months into training with her new horse, Claire was finally ready to ride over to Tessa's neighborhood and meet the Idylwild Cowgirls. However, one large obstacle separated the girls - Paynes Prairie - a two-mile wide marsh that is inhabited by hundreds of snakes and alligators. Paynes Prairie could be crossed. In fact, hundreds of cars zipped across the Prairie every day on Highway 441. And the grassy shoulder next to the pavement was wide enough for her to traverse the Prairie by horseback.

The girls agreed to leave their houses at 8:30 the following morning and meet midway along the Paynes Prairie crossing.

"Why don't you spend the night so we can ride together the next day before you head back home?" Tessa asked Claire.

"Sure," Claire agreed, "but where will I keep Shotsie?"

"He can stay in the pasture with my two horses. It's big enough for all three."

Claire awoke early the next morning with a jolt of adrenaline. She rushed through breakfast and stuffed a change of clothes into her backpack. She hurried out to the pasture, almost skipping through the dew-covered grass. As she reached the chestnut, she noticed his coat shining as red and glorious as the morning sun. She buckled the halter around his face, gently stroked his neck, and whispered, "We're going on an adventure today, our first ride north. We'll meet Tessa and her friends. I

## Chapter 5

know you'll be brave and I'll keep a keen lookout for snakes as we cross the Prairie."

The pair set off on their excursion. They trotted down the long driveway that ushered them to the four-lane, with Shotsie's ears cast forward and Claire giddy with excitement. When they reached Highway 441, they turned right and traveled north along the mowed shoulder. They set their sights toward Gainesville and the Idylwild Cowgirls. As they approached the Prairie, the road and its adjoining grassy edge abruptly descended a natural escarpment to the level green savannah that defined Paynes Prairie.

Many mornings when Claire had crossed the Prairie as a passenger in her parent's station wagon, she saw a thick wedge of fog clinging to the low-lying marsh. But this morning was different. The air was clear, the sky a cerulean blue, and visibility restricted only by the limitations of one's eyes.

High on her horse's back, Claire could see clear across the Prairie to the far tree line that defined the north boundary. Looking east into the untamed wetland, she gazed at the waterscape beyond. She marveled at the expanse of yellow and purple marsh flowers – water lotus and pickerelweed – that painted the otherwise green savannah a rainbow of colors.

Surrounded by the colorful bog plants was a large stand of shrubs - willows, myrtles, and elderberry bushes – that was alive with birds. The bird rookery was situated about 500 feet beyond the road clearing, and it was the same rookery she'd seen when she crossed the Prairie in her parent's car. But this time, she viewed it slowly. She stared at the perpetual comings and goings of the parent birds as they flew in and out of the avian nursery where hundreds of baby birds were being raised. And she delighted at the loud chatter that arose from the birds' breeding ground.

She continued her journey north, and a half hour later, she spotted a large, white van slowing down and easing off the highway onto the grassy edge. The doors opened and eight or nine people piled out. As she approached, she saw several passengers holding buckets and long-handled nets, and she could see faded letters on the side of the van that read, "UF."

A young man with shoulder-length dark hair called out. "Hey Dr. Carr, how many buckets do you think we'll need?"

"Grab them all," replied a clean-cut older man with sharply chiseled facial features. "We're heading way out into the marsh and we don't want to come back for more buckets."

Claire halted her horse and watched the controlled commotion.

One of the students waved and greeted her. "Hi there. Nice horse you have."

Claire waved back as she glanced down proudly at the chestnut whose ears were alert to the surrounding activity. "Thanks," she replied. Then Claire gestured toward the equipment. "What kind of sampling are y'all doing?"

Before the student could answer, the professor approached. "Hola Señorita," he said in an animated but kind voice. "My, what a magnificent animal you're riding." He grinned as he gestured toward the students milling around the white van. "This is my field zoology class from the University, and we're going to inventory the critters out here on the Prairie - the fish, reptiles, and amphibians."

Claire nodded and then pointed behind her. "Did you see all of the birds back there? I can't believe how noisy they are."

"Yes, that is a rookery of egrets, mostly cattle egrets," the professor explained. "But herons and ibis and anhingas are nesting there too."

## Chapter 5

"Why did they pick those small trees so close to the highway to build their nests in?"

The professor grinned as he geared his explanation to the young teenager instead of his college class. "Those birds are real smart, and they have a deal with the alligators. They build their nests where there are lots of small trees that will hold all those nests. And the trees have to be in fairly deep water so the gators can patrol the rookery."

Claire wrinkled her brow as she pondered why the birds would want to nest near alligators.

The professor noticed Claire's confusion. "Raccoons and other predators love to eat eggs and baby birds, and a few raccoons could wipe out an entire colony of nesting birds overnight if they can get to it. But if there are alligators in the water, the raccoons won't swim out to the rookery, or they'll be eaten."

Claire nodded at the professor's explanation. "Pretty smart of the birds to build their nests where the gators will protect 'em."

"The alligators benefit too. They will eat any young birds that fall from the nests and any predators that try to swim out to the rookery."

Claire grinned at the man and then nudged her horse forward. "Nice to talk to you and thanks for the information. I am on my way to meet a friend."

"We saw five girls on horses a couple miles back," said one of the male students who had paused to listen to his professor's explanation. "They were headed this way."

Claire waved to the group and continued her journey north along the highway's wide, grassy edge. She marveled at the sights and sounds of the Prairie, an experience missed by all who dashed across the expansive wetland by car. Shotsie perked up both ears, arched his neck slightly, and announced in his quiet yet animated language that he detected movement ahead.

Four girls were riding with Tessa. When Claire finally converged with the others, Tessa made the introductions. "That's Andi on the tall Appaloosa and Jodi on the smallest horse. And that's Kris, the one with glasses, and her little sister, LeeAnne."

LeeAnne grimaced as she pushed the unruly curls from her face. "Why do I haff to be Kwis's wittle sistuh? Why can't I just be LeeAnne?"

Tessa looked at the youngest cowgirl and whispered, "Sorry," which caused LeeAnne to respond with a sheepish smile.

"Howdy everyone," Claire said as she greeted the group.

Tessa gestured over at Jodi. "Jodi's getting a horse soon. But in the meantime, she's ridin' my pony, Snuffy."

"Yep," Jodi nodded. "I'm gettin' a horse right when we finish building the fence."

And with those introductions, the young cowgirls reined their mounts north, with Claire and Shotsie charting new territory, and the others reversing their initial course.

## Chapter 6

Chatting continuously like birds at the rookery, the girls shared horse stories as they journeyed along the grassy shoulder of Highway 441. After a while, the horses halted abruptly, perked up their ears, and jerked their heads to the right. The horses detected a sound or perhaps a movement that the animated girls had not.

The cowgirls wondered what had attracted their horses' attention, and soon heard a faint whinny. A line of apartment buildings straddled both sides of a paved entrance road, and a sign by the highway read 'Prairie View Apartments'.

Kris looked puzzled. "Why would there be a horse in that apartment complex?"

"I don't know," Andi replied. "Let's take a look."

The girls reined their mounts toward the red brick apartments in search of the mystery horse. It wasn't long before they found the source of the whinny. A buckskin-colored mare with a narrow white blaze was tied to an oak tree in front of one of the apartment buildings.

"Look at that poor horse!" Jodi exclaimed. "Someone tied it to a tree, and it's all tangled up."

"Oh no," LeeAnne gasped. "It doesn't have any watuh, eithuh. We've got to help it."

Jodi slid off the pony and handed the reins to Tessa. "I'll untangle it."

LeeAnne dismounted too. "I'll help you."

"You poor thing," Jodi mumbled as she untangled the long rope, first from around the horse's front leg and then from around the tree. Then she noticed the injury. "The rope's cut your leg."

LeeAnne cringed as she glimpsed the wound. "You shuh have a cwuel ownuh."

At that moment, the door of Apartment D-8 opened, and a middle-aged man wearing suspenders, a dirty shirt, and old blue jeans emerged from the building. "What's goin' on out here?" he growled as he looked around at the cavalry that surrounded his horse. Then he focused on the two girls next to the mare. "What are you doing with my horse?"

LeeAnne lowered her shoulders and cast her eyes to the ground. She didn't care that her unruly ringlets covered her eyes. The man was frightening.

Andi was not fazed by the man's hostility. She squared her shoulders and shot right back. "Your horse was all tangled up, so they just freed her. That's all."

Kris pushed up her glasses, a habit she had when she was nervous, and tried to explain why her little sister was holding onto the horse's rope. Sympathy seeped into her trembling voice. "LeeAnne was just trying to help the poor horse."

Jodi gathered her courage as she stood up next to LeeAnne. "The horse doesn't have any water. How is it supposed to drink or graze when it's tied to a tree?"

The man put his hands on his hips and barked back. "How I care for my horse ain't none of your business."

Tessa, the peace-keeper in the group, tried to calm the stranger. "Sir, we really weren't trying to take your horse, we were just untangling it."

*Chapter 6*

The man gazed at the group that was huddled around his horse. His voice softened. "Well, I uh, appreciate you untanglin' my horse. She ain't really my horse," he began to explain. "She was my brother's horse, but he moved to Atlanta, so he dumped her off here. I'm gonna turn her loose on Paynes Prairie so she can fend for herself."

The girls stared at the man, not sure how to respond. Claire finally broke the silence. "Mister, how old is the horse and has it ever been ridden?"

"Well, let's see," the man thought as he raised his hand to his chin. "I remember my brother sayin' that she's two or three, or maybe four by now. He bought the horse for his daughter to ride, but Tina was too young, so my brother would lift her up onto the horse's back and lead them around the pasture. The horse didn't seem to mind, even when Tina got all excited and kicked her legs. That horse must'a known there was a youngin on her back 'cause she stayed calm, just like she was babysittin' little Tina."

Kris spoke up again, this time with more confidence as she offered up a solution. "Mister, what if we give you $15 for the horse and take her off your hands right now?" She gestured toward Jodi who was standing next to the buckskin. "Jodi there needs a horse real bad, and this horse might just fit the bill."

Jodi was stunned. She turned to Kris and stuttered. "But, but I don't have $15 dollars. I don't even know if I can ride the horse. And where will I keep her until I finish building my fence? And besides, what will my parents say about me bringing a horse home today?"

"You can keep her in Mr. Taylor's pasture," Kris offered.

"But shouldn't I ask him first?"

Andi shook her head. "No, his pasture's all grown up with weeds. He won't even know she's out there."

Kris offered another solution. "We can all help you build your fence by digging more post holes every day. That way you can get your fence built sooner."

"Maybe my daddy'll come over again after work and help too," Tessa suggested.

*Chapter 6*

Jodi looked around at her new friends who were all staring back at her. She started to panic. How could they so unexpectedly throw a horse her way? Shouldn't she have a say in which horse she gets? She managed to voice one of her many worries. "How, how will I pay for the horse?" she stuttered. "I don't even have one dollar with me."

This time the man answered even though she had directed the questions to her friends. "You can sign an IOU that says you'll pay me $15 within one week."

Tessa looked at the stranger. "Can she return the horse if her parents won't let her keep it?"

"Yeah, I guess so," he answered.

Kris grinned at Jodi. "I guess you just got yourself a horse."

Jodi was shocked, speechless. She had wanted a horse for years, dreaming of that magical day. But time seemed to move so slowly, or rather, the time to finish building her fence so she could start looking for a horse seemed to take forever. Then unexpectedly, in the span of a few minutes, she was holding a rope that was attached to a horse that now belonged to her. That was of course if her parents let her keep it.

The man wrote out an IOU stating that Jodi would pay $15 within a week for the buckskin mare. He signed the sheet and added his phone number.

Jodi tried to read the note, but her eyes swelled with tears and blurred her vision. All she could think to say was, "Mister, what's her name?"

"She don't have a name, not that I know of," he replied. "I only heard my brother call her 'The Horse'. I guess you get to name her."

Tessa suggested they lead the young mare over to her house so they could feed and water her and clean the wound on her ankle. Then they would take her to Mr. Taylor's pasture and turn her out with the cows and other horses.

Jodi slowly rolled up the long, frayed rope that was attached to her very own horse as she tried to comprehend her new acquisition. The procession departed the Prairie View Apartments, with Tessa ponying Jodi's earlier mount, and Jodi leading her newly acquired horse.

After a spell, Andi called back to Jodi from her lead position. "I don't know who has a bigger smile, you cause you just got yourself a new horse or the horse cause she ain't tied to a tree and tangled up no more. I think you done rescued each other!"

The other cowgirls grinned and warmed at the thought of their new friend with her very own horse.

When they reached Tessa's house, Tessa motioned to Jodi. "Lead your horse over to the water trough. When she's through drinking, bring her to the barn, and we'll clean her wound."

Tessa brought out a plastic bottle that contained a copper-colored liquid. "This is betadine. We'll clean her cut with it," she explained, "and then run water slowly over the sore to flush out any dirt that's stuck in it."

"Should we bandage her ankle?" Jodi asked.

"No," Andi replied. "Best to let it air so it'll heal faster."

"I want to bathe her and wash off all the dirt and sweat," Jodi said as she acknowledged the buckskin's unkempt condition.

The girls joined Jodi in cleaning and medicating the new horse. They washed her entire body with a curry, a sponge, and a bucket full of soapy water. Tessa retrieved a bottle of hair conditioner from her parent's shower and squirted half of the container into the mare's knotted mane and tail. After the

*Chapter 6*

conditioner thoroughly penetrated the matted mess, the girls combed out the tangles.

At that moment, Tessa's father emerged from his workshop. He looked at the girls huddled around the new horse and shook his head. "I do declare. That is one lucky horse to have all you youngins fussin' over her. When I die," he chuckled, "I want to be reincarnated as that horse right there."

The recently rescued horse was now the cleanest animal at the barn, and since she'd just been scrubbed from head to hoof, she should have sparkled. But no amount of soaping and scouring could overcome her dull, coarse coat, protruding ribs, and cracked hooves. Months of disregard and neglect couldn't be erased by just one cleaning. What she needed now was to be dewormed, her hooves trimmed, a nutritious diet, and a loving, caring owner. Jodi was ready to accept this challenge. What worried her was whether her parents would agree.

Jodi handed the lead rope to Tessa. "Will you hold her while I climb on her back?"

"Sure. You can use the mounting block over there."

Jodi gently lifted her right leg up and eased it over the horse's back. The horse tensed and cocked both ears back. Jodi sat motionlessly, and then instinctively began to caress the mare's neck and mane and withers. "I decided on a name," Jodi announced while sitting on her new horse. "Scout, like Tonto the Indian's horse. She's not a paint like Tonto's horse, but she seems brave and I bet she's fast, or at least she will be once her ankle heals. And I just know she will be kind and full of heart."

Kris nudged up her glasses and nodded. "Scout's a mighty fine name." And the other girls agreed.

The girls rode to Mr. Taylor's pasture while Jodi followed behind leading her new horse. Twenty minutes and one country mile later, they arrived at their destination.

"Are you sure I can keep Scout here?" Jodi asked.

Kris was adamant. "Sure, Mr. Taylor won't even notice."

"What's he gonna do anyway?" Andi sassed. "He wouldn't evict your horse and toss her out onto Rocky Point Road."

"It's only for a few days til your fence is done," Kris reassured her.

Jodi ushered the buckskin through the gate. The visiting horse caught sight of the herd on the far side of the pasture. Whinnies were exchanged. The resident horses pranced over to Scout and greeted her with snorts and more whinnies. The cowgirls watched from outside the fence as two of the horses sparred with their front hooves, while the third turned and kicked out with both hind legs. Scout bolted sideways and avoided the kick. Several more minutes passed of sniffing each other, trotting around the pasture, snorting, and more whinnies before the horses began to accept the newcomer into the herd.

The girls were leaving Mr. Taylor's pasture when a tall, athletic girl with a paper bag tucked under her arm ran up to the gate. Andi greeted the runner. "Hi, Gina."

"Howdy," Gina replied as she wiped the sweat from her brow. "What are y'all up to?"

Andi gestured to Jodi, who was the only girl not sitting on a horse. "That's Jodi, and she got a new horse today. We just turned it out into the pasture."

Jodi pointed to the group of still-excited horses. "That's her over there, the buckskin. Her name's Scout," she said apprehensively, not fully accepting her new acquisition.

The girls recounted the rescue. They explained how they were all helping to build a fence for the new horse, except that Jodi's parents didn't know about Scout yet.

"That's why we're hidin' her here for a few days," Kris explained.

*Chapter 6*

"Are you gonna ride your horse?" Tessa asked Gina.

"Yep," Gina replied.

Gina coaxed her horse away from the excited herd with a handful of sweet feed. She groomed and bridled the gelding while the other girls waited, and then swung up on him bareback. The band of girls departed together, with Jodi riding tandem with Tessa since she was leaving her new horse behind.

Jodi wanted to learn more about Gina. "How far do you run to get to the pasture?" she asked.

"A mile and a half," Gina replied.

"That's a long way, don't you have a bicycle?" Jodi asked.

"Yeah, I ride my bike over here sometimes, but I prefer to run. I'm on the soccer team at Gainesville High, and running here every day keeps me in shape for the team. Since Mr. Taylor only charges me $5 dollars a month to keep my horse here, I figure the price is right, and I will keep up the long commute."

"We can go to your house this afternoon and dig more post holes," Tessa offered to Jodi. "Maybe my dad'll even come over and help us."

"Won't my daddy be surprised when he comes home from work and sees all of us working on the fence," Jodi laughed.

"Not as surprised as when you tell him you already got a horse to put inside the new fence," Andi joked.

Jodi fell silent as she thought of bringing her new horse home and the obstacles she first had to overcome.

Claire inadvertently interrupted Jodi's thoughts. "I can help you train Scout." Claire described the horse training techniques that she was learning from her instructor. "I could teach you those things too."

Jodi marveled at her new friends. She could never have imagined she would meet such a friendly group of cowgirls, girls who would help build a fence, find her a horse, and teach her how to train her new horse. Now if they would only convince her parents to let her keep the new horse. Jodi decided she wasn't brave enough to reveal her secret to her parents. She still had six days before her debt became due, almost a week to figure out a strategy.

## Chapter 7

Claire spent the night at Tessa's house, and after a second day of riding with the cowgirls, she departed on her journey south back to her home. Tessa and the others accompanied her part way across Paynes Prairie. Then they bid her farewell as they retreated northward back to their Idylwild neighborhood.

As Claire continued alone across the edge of the Prairie, she reached down and stroked her mount's soft, chestnut coat. She was proud of how well Shotsie behaved on their first journey away from home, and how he'd accepted the unfamiliar sights and new horses. Then she recalled the bird rookery up ahead, and the birds' loud chatter and constant flights as they retrieved and delivered food to the nestlings.

She squinted and raised her hand to her brow as she searched for the island of shrubs that housed the birds' nests. Even though the rookery was still several hundred yards away, she could see parent birds winging across the expansive marsh. She noticed the white birds, mostly cattle egrets as she'd learned from Dr. Carr, with their dark orange bill and light orange crest. She searched for other birds too, the less common ones, and spotted some that were blue and some that were black and still others that were a multitude of colors. As she searched for different birds, any species that deviated in color or size from the almost all white egrets, her eyes latched onto another deviation, a pattern that marked a sharp departure from the uniformly mowed grass that surrounded her.

Unfurled beside her was a giant snake that stretched a full horse length in size. Claire's eyes first locked onto the serpent's massive girth. She noticed the leather-colored diamonds that repeated along the entire length of its back until the pattern terminated with a string full of rattles. The reptile was a poisonous diamondback rattlesnake, and it was lying only a foot from their walking path, parallel to the direction that she and her horse were traveling.

The serpent didn't move as she passed by. Perhaps it was not threatened by the gentle equine and his timid rider. After all, it was top predator within nature's complex food web. Or perhaps it was full from a recent meal and not willing to budge, for it never acknowledged the horse and rider, and likewise, the horse did not react.

But Claire reacted. She gasped, her entire body tensed, and then she began to cry as fear overwhelmed her. However, the danger was over by the time the tears spilled onto her cheeks, for the horse and rider had passed by the deadly reptile unharmed.

Claire spotted a man standing in the grassy right-of-way up ahead. He was holding something dark and looking east toward the bird rookery. When he lifted the object to his face, she realized he was gazing at the birds through a pair of binoculars. She struggled to compose herself as she approached the birdwatcher.

"Howdy," the man said as he turned to greet her. "Pretty horse you got there."

Claire attempted a smile, but she was still unsettled. She sniffed and pretended she was swatting at a bug rather than wiping away a tear. Then she noticed the man's blue baseball

*Chapter 7*

cap with a silhouette of a bird that resembled an egret at the rookery. His wavy black hair emerged from under his cap and almost touched the shoulders of his broad, strong frame. He was smiling, and she noticed his large brown eyes that projected both excitement and kindness. He gestured toward the thicket of shrubs that was the source of the bird sounds. "Did you notice the rookery over there?"

"Yeah, I did," she replied, hoping he wouldn't notice her tear-stained face or her still-trembling hands. "Are you looking at the birds?"

"Yep, I'm monitoring the birds in the rookery for the new State Park."

"Are you a bird scientist?"

"Nope," he grinned, "just a guy who likes to watch birds. The park hasn't hired a biologist yet, so they don't have anyone to monitor the rookery."

"Have you monitored birds before?"

"Not really, at least not for scientific purposes," he answered as he resumed scanning back and forth with his binoculars. "But I've been watching birds for a long time, about 15 years."

"That's a long time." She didn't acknowledge that she was only 13. "You must have started when you were real young."

The man lowered his binoculars to reply, and when he looked over at Claire, his dark eyes danced with excitement. "Yep, when I was eight-years-old, the two ladies who lived next door took me bird watching. And I've been doing it ever since," he beamed.

Claire figured that bird watching produced that same thrill for him that she experienced every time she stepped into the stirrup and hoisted her body onto the back of her four-legged friend.

He walked over and extended his hand. "My name is John, John Hintermister the fifth."

She reached down and shook his hand. "I'm Claire Hill, and this is Shotsie. We live a few miles south of here."

"Shotsie," he grinned. "He's a real pretty horse. That big white face of his is like a headlamp. You can't sneak up on anyone with a face as bright as his. I could see you coming from a mile away."

Claire's stomach tightened. "Well, tell that to the scary rattlesnake we just snuck up on. It was as long as my horse and real fat too."

"Wow, a diamondback rattlesnake," he grinned as he slowly emphasized each word. "I wonder if it just ate a rabbit. Gosh, a snake that size could swallow a small gator." He paused a moment as if to ponder whether the venomous viper could actually ingest an alligator. "You know what we need here?"

"What?"

"An underpass so all the snakes and other animals can cross under the highway and not get run over. Just think how many are killed every week and every year as they try to cross the road."

Claire shuddered. She didn't want to think about all those snakes, so she changed to a more pleasant topic. "Tell me more about the bird rookery."

John was happy to oblige. "Cattle egrets are the most abundant type of bird in the rookery. There are also snowy egrets and white ibis, and little blue herons, Louisiana herons, and anhingas. I've seen a few green herons and a couple of black-crowned night herons dart in and out of the shrubs, so I assume they're nesting there too. That makes at least eight species. Other rookeries I've seen or heard about only have

*Chapter 7*

three or four or maybe five species, and there aren't as many nests as this one has. That's why this rookery is so important."

The bird watcher's enthusiasm was contagious, and Claire nodded in fascination as she listened to his description. "Thank you for telling me so much about the birds. I'm gonna come back here with my parents' binoculars so I can look at them more closely." She waved as she nudged her mount forward. "Nice to meet you, Mr. John. I need to head home."

"See ya," he waved.

The young equestrian resumed her journey south, her mind filled with the chatter of the rookery and her new knowledge of the nesting birds.

## Chapter 8

Four of the cowgirls – Andi, Kris, LeeAnne, and Tessa – had accompanied Claire part-way across the Prairie before they turned back north toward their rural Idylwild neighborhood. Jodi had not joined them on this ride.

Kris reached down and twisted her fingers around her mare's silky mane. "Jodi has a new horse, but no tack or equipment or even horse feed to fatten up skinny-ole-Scout."

"It's not like she can ask her parents to buy that stuff, not until she tells 'em she has a horse," Andi replied as she looked back at Kris from her lead position.

"But none of us have spare horse supplies to give her," Tessa added. "My parents don't buy me anything extra. They can barely afford the sweet feed and hay."

"I have an idea," Kris exclaimed as she nudged up her glasses. "We can all loan Jodi a horse item – a brush, bucket, hoof pick, or maybe a bridle – just for her to borrow. She can return them as soon as she gets her own tack and supplies."

"Yeah, and we can ask everyone to donate one scoop of horse feed, or whatever they can spare, to *Jodi's Skinny Horse Cause*," Andi suggested. "We'll combine all the feed together into one bucket for Scout. She sure needs some grain to help cover her bony ribs."

*Chapter 8*

With their plan in place, the girls agreed to bring their loaner items and a scoop of horse feed to Tessa's house the next day for Jodi to retrieve.

As the cowgirls drifted leisurely along their treasured Crown Road, two neighborhood boys rocketed up on their motorbikes. They pulled alongside the girls and revved their motors.

Kris shouted over the loud rumbling. "What are you trying to prove?"

"Oh nothing, Four Eyes," Toby shot back as he sneered at Kris and downshifted to neutral.

LeeAnne giggled when she heard the boy call her sister, 'Four Eyes'.

The girls reined their horses to a halt and Tessa looked down at the two boys. Although they were older, perhaps 15 and 16, and certainly much larger than the small petite equestrian, Tessa towered over the boys as she perched high up on her long-legged palomino. She shouted to be heard. "Did you know Mr. Moody's trying to get the county to widen and pave this here dirt road?"

"Yep," Ben, the younger of the two, nodded. "My parents don't want it done, and neither do we."

"Our parents don't want it either," Andi said.

"Then why don't you round up your cowgirl friends and tell Mr. Moody how much you hate his idea?" Toby scowled.

"Why don't you?" Kris shot back.

"Tell you what," Toby suggested as he turned to the younger boy and smirked. "Let's race, motorbikes against horses. Losers have to tell Mr. Moody that we're all against widenin' and pavin' Crown Road."

"Deal," Andi agreed before any of the other cowgirls could reply. "We'll meet you at Weidemeyer Road in one hour and race you there." Andi was eager to accept this challenge, especially from the annoying motorbike boys. She was bold, a risk-taker, and unconventional in her riding habits. The maneuvers she coaxed her horse to execute far exceeded what most well-trained horses were willing to do for their riders. Andi was the personification of horse-riding adventures and it affected all of her cowgirl friends.

Ben nodded in agreement. "We'll be there."

The boys revved their motors, shifted into gear, and sped off, leaving a cloud of dust and plume of exhaust.

Tessa closed her eyes and waved her hand in front of her face. "I don't know what's more obnoxious, those boys or their motorbikes?"

"Both," Andi and Kris said in unison.

Tessa felt her body sag as she turned to Andi. "You're the only one of us who has a chance of beatin' those boys."

Andi lifted her shoulders. "Bingo and I'll give 'em a run for their money. Gina's horse is pretty fast too. Let's see if she's home and maybe she'll race 'em with me."

Kris pushed up the rim of her glasses. "Those boys would just as soon run Patches and me over as race us."

LeeAnne giggled as she recalled the rodeo and her sister's bucking bronco. "That was vewy funny seein' Patches thow 'em off."

"Yeah, and he's been mean ever since," Kris said.

*Chapter 8*

"Or just tryin' to get even," Tessa added in a more serious tone.

The girls continued west along Crown Road until they reached the woods trail that led them to the houses by the school. They found Gina at home and asked if she would participate in the impromptu race with the motorbike boys.

"Sure," Gina agreed. "I'll ride my bike over to Mr. Taylor's pasture and get Buck. I'll meet you at Power Line Road in a half hour."

Power Line Road was not an actual road, but a mowed grassy strip that wove under the towering electrical structures that crisscrossed the northwest corner of their rural neighborhood. Like the other neighbors, the cowgirls used the mowed right-of-way as a connector route to reach destinations north of their Idylwild neighborhood.

The four girls were waiting at the south end of Power Line Road when Gina cantered up. After they converged, the cowgirls-turned-jockeys trotted their horses along the grassy lane, with Andi and Gina in front, Tessa and Kris in the middle of the pack, and young LeeAnne trailing behind. When they approached a curve, Kris sprinted her pony ahead and sliced between the two front riders.

"Bet you can't catch me!" Kris called out as she passed the two leaders.

Andi shot Gina a conspiratory glance and pointed at Kris. Gina nodded, and the two galloped up to Kris. When they caught up with her, the two girls reached down and grabbed Kris's arms and lifted her straight up.

"Put me down, put me down!" Kris shouted as she maintained a tight grip on the reins but lost complete seat contact with her mount.

*The Idylwild Cowgirls*

Confused but unwavering, the pinto continued her riderless canter, flanked on both sides by the two taller horses. After five or six strides of suspending Kris above her horse, Andi and Gina lowered Kris back onto her cantering pony. Then, without missing a stride, the two jokester jockeys squeezed their horses to a gallop. When they approached the final curve along Power

*Chapter 8*

Line Road, they reined their horses to a walk so the others could catch up.

Tessa was still laughing after having witnessed Kris's temporary departure from the saddle. "That was the funniest thing I've ever seen!"

"Yeah, and it suhves you wight Kwis fuh all the mean fings you've done to me," LeeAnne said to her older sister.

"Well I didn't think it was so funny," Kris countered. "But you sure left Patches and me in the dust back there."

Andi's grin stretched from one beet-red check to the other as she glanced over at Kris. Of all the cowgirls, Kris was her favorite riding buddy, and consequently, the most frequent recipient of her many pranks.

The girls reined their horses north toward Weidemeyer Road and arrived at the makeshift race track before their challengers. The boys' arrival was announced by the advancing roar of motorbikes.

Straight, grassy, and remote, Weidemeyer Road was the cowgirls' preferred galloping track. There they pretended to be jockeys, crouched over the withers of their lightning-fast thoroughbreds, hands sawing back and forth in rhythm to the galloping hooves, while staring through the middle of their horses' pricked ears. The equestrians had raced each other at Weidemeyer Road, but they had never raced the motorbike riders.

The competitors assembled at the south end of the road next to the cattle pasture and discussed the rules of the race. They settled on racing in the grassy sides of the dirt road rather than the sandy ruts. Although the grass was tall and overgrown, it would suffice for this impromptu neighborhood race.

The group decided that the two jockeys, Andi and Gina, would run on the right side of the dirt road while their opponents raced on the left side. Kris offered to stand at the starting line and signal the rivals to begin. Tessa and LeeAnne rode ahead to the finish line so they could determine the race's winner. The finish line corresponded to the north end of a cow pasture, a racing length of about two furlongs, or a quarter of a mile.

When Tessa and LeeAnne reached the finish line and positioned themselves along the edge of the grassy lane, Tessa waved back and yelled, "Ready anytime you are!"

From her pinto's back, Kris signaled that she had received the message. Facing the competitors, the two jockeys on her left and the two motorists on her right, she reached up and pulled the red bandanna off her head. She waved the scarf and yelled, "Riders ready, riders to your mark, riders go!" And on the word 'go', she snapped the bandanna to her waist.

The two horses surged forward in response to their riders' sharp kicks and loud shouts and the simultaneous roar of the nearby motorbikes.

"Come on, Bingo!" Andi yelled, as she crouched over his withers and stretched her arms forward. "You can beat those boys!" The Appaloosa lowered his head, ears flicking back and forth, as his hooves pounded at top speed against the grassy turf. Andi felt a bolt of pure joy as she galloped down the makeshift racetrack.

Toby and Ben soon pulled ahead of the jockeys and became the front runners in the mismatched race. Determined and unwavering, the girls continued galloping in an all-out effort to catch up with the motorcycles. As the finish line approached, the boys abruptly decelerated and steered their bikes sharply toward the sandy ruts in the center of the track. When the bikes slowed and took evasive action, the two jockeys surged ahead. Andi crossed the finish line first, two strides ahead of Gina and four strides in front of the motorbikes.

*Chapter 8*

Toby angled over to the referees. "No fair!" he shouted as he raised his shoulders from the crouched position and waved his arm. "There was a log in our way!"

"You should'a jumped the log!" Tessa hollered back.

LeeAnne joined in the shouting match. "Yeah, owuh hohses would have jumped the wog, so you should've too!"

"You lost the race!" Tessa announced authoritatively. "The horses beat you fair and square! You boys have to ask Mr. Moody to not develop our dirt road!"

Ben shook his head in protest. "Since that log stopped us from winning the race, I think we should all tell Mr. Moody."

The two jockeys reined up their horses and trotted back to the quarreling group. Andi, the official winner, reached down and victoriously slapped her champion, Bingo, who was drenched in sweat and heaving back and forth. Andi grinned triumphantly as she approached the group.

"Yeah, the boys are right," Andi agreed. "There's power in numbers. Let's all visit Mr. Moody together."

"Oh, ok," Tessa acquiesced.

"Well, what are we waiting for?" Andi asked to no one in particular. "Let's head over there right now!"

## Chapter 9

The boys rocketed ahead to Mr. Moody's house to separate themselves from the cowgirls, who ambled more slowly as they relished their victory. The girls followed Power Line Road under the towering electrical structures and past the blackberry bushes.

"Don't get any ideas," Kris warned her two prankster friends as she held tight to her horse's mane and shot them a rebellious glance.

"What?" Andi asked innocently. "You don't trust us very much, do you?"

"I know you always have some kind of prank up your sleeve," Kris replied.

LeeAnne giggled at her older sister's vexation.

They followed the path through the woods to Crown Road and then to the entrance of Mr. Moody's farm. Toby and Ben were waiting for them next to the owner's mailbox.

"What took y'all so long?" Toby asked the girls as he sat idling his motorbike.

"Y'all sure are slow," Ben added.

"We're fast when it counts," Andi shot back.

Gina grinned. "And we know how to jump over logs."

LeeAnne giggled at the verbal sparring until Tessa spoke up. "OK now. Let's quit picking at each other and ride up to

*Chapter 9*

Mr. Moody's house together. We gotta tell him how upset we all are at the possibility of losing our dirt road."

The two boys revved their motorbikes, and Ben popped the clutch causing the bike to fishtail back and forth and sending dirt spraying into the air.

LeeAnne shielded her eyes and tried to prevent the soil from hitting her face. "He shuh is mean!" she said as she pushed the persistent ringlets from her eyes.

"Just a sore loser," Tessa replied.

The girls trotted down Mr. Moody's driveway to the white brick house that sat nestled under a stand of hardwood trees. Green shutters bookmarked both front windows, and several pots of red flowers decorated the front porch. A rooster crowed in the back yard.

"Looks like a real nice place to live," Kris observed.

"I don't know why he'd want to turn his peaceful farm into a housin' development," Tessa said.

"Money," Andi replied.

Gina looked at the two boys who were straddling their still-idling motorbikes. "You lost the race, you ring the doorbell," she directed.

Hesitantly, Toby turned off the motor and shuffled toward the front door. As he approached the porch, the door opened, and a short, broad man filled the doorway.

The owner was momentarily startled to see a boy walking toward him. He opened the screen door to see who else had gathered in his front yard. He shoved his hands into his jeans and looked around at the crowd of teenagers perched on their horses and motorbikes. "What can I do for you today?" he asked in a low baritone.

His question was met with silence as the seven teenagers tried to decide who would speak first. Then four started speaking at once, with Andi winning out with her domineering voice. "We love Crown Road just the way it is, and we don't want it widened and paved," she announced authoritatively.

"How will we ride our horses on the road if you pave it?" Gina asked.

"We want to keep the neighborhood peaceful and quiet just like it is now," Tessa insisted.

"And if you cut down all those big twees, wheuh will all the squhhels and buwds wiv?" LeeAnne squeaked.

"You have one of the most beautiful farms on all of Crown Road," Kris said as she gestured at the landscape surrounding them. "Why would you want to destroy all of this and build houses on it?"

Ben and Toby stood mute as they looked from girl to girl. They may have lost the race, but the cowgirls were the ones interrogating Mr. Moody.

"Well now," Mr. Moody began as he cut off the next speaker. "I see why y'all are paying me a visit." He cleared his throat as he again scanned the crowd who had gathered in his front yard. "Y'all ain't the only ones against my development. Some of the other neighbors called me up to complain. But you youngins just don't understand the power of money. And believe me, I won't be the only one to profit. All the farms and houses on this here road will be worth a lot more if we improve that dusty, pothole-ridden dirt road. So y'all just run along now and mind your own business."

Feeling defeated, the cowgirls dropped their shoulders, hung their heads, and turned to leave. But Andi hesitated. She straightened her back and reined her mount around to face the developer. "We'll find some way to stop you!" she threatened. "You'll see!"

# Chapter 10

Jodi secretly gathered up items from around her house for her horse-in-hiding - a bath cloth, bucket, and bar of soap to cleanse the ankle abrasion and wash Scout's entire body; a rarely-used hairbrush for combing out the tangles in the mare's mane and tail; a dog brush for grooming her coat; and a treat for Scout, two carrots that she hoped her mom wouldn't notice missing. It wasn't much, but it would do for now. She stuffed the items into her brother's backpack, hopped on her bike, and pedaled over to Tessa's house.

Tessa greeted Jodi when she arrived. "Come see what we got for you!"

Jodi propped her bike against a tree and followed Tessa to the tack room.

"Ta da!" Tessa said as she opened the barn door and presented Jodi was a stack of horse items. "These are for you," she announced.

Jodi stared at the collection of items and was speechless as she tried to comprehend the kindness of her new friends. She picked up the green horse brush and slowly stroked the bristles across her arm. She lifted the braided white lead rope and fingered the metal clasp. A lone tear trickled down her cheek as she caressed the soft foam on the blue bareback pad. She turned to her friend and in a barely audible voice, stuttered, "Are, are these for Scout and me?"

Tessa grinned and nodded. "Yep, they're all loaner items to help you get started with your new horse, all except the horse food, which is yours to keep and feed to Scout." Tessa gestured at the bareback pad and bridle. "Charlene's away for the summer so her mom said we could borrow these until she returns. That way you'll have some tack to start riding with."

Jodi looked over the items again. "Y'all are the nicest friends I've ever had."

Tessa laughed. "Come on. Let's go see your new horse."

Jodi gathered some of the loaner gifts and stuffed them into her brother's Scooby-doo pack. She poured a generous ration of horse feed into the bucket. "Scout's gonna love this," she grinned.

Tessa retrieved her bike from the back shed, and the two girls set off on their mile-long commute to Mr. Taylor's pasture. Jodi wore the backpack full of horse supplies and balanced a bucket of horse feed on the handlebars, right next to the sagging wicker basket that was still ripped from her bike wreck not too long ago.

The girls arrived at the pasture to find Scout grazing on the far side of the field with the resident herd. "I'll take her a carrot so she's easier to catch," Jodi said as she propped her bike against the fence and removed the bucket of feed from the handlebars.

"Don't let the other horses see you give her a carrot or they won't leave you alone," Tessa advised. "I'll walk out with you and try to keep 'em away."

Jodi snuck Scout a carrot while Tessa distracted the other horses. They led the recently rescued horse back to the gate so they could groom, medicate, and simply fuss over her. The small herd trailed behind the newcomer but soon lost interest.

*Chapter 10*

The girls bathed Scout, cleaned her wound, and picked her hooves.

"Wanna ride her around the pasture and see how she does?' Tessa asked.

Jodi hesitated. "Oh, I don't know if I should ride her bareback out here with the other horses around."

"How about I lead her around while you just sit on her?" Tessa offered. "I'll keep her away from the other horses."

"Ok," Jodi agreed. "I sure do want to start ridin' her."

The rescued mare was not as compliant as the girls had hoped. She halted and hesitantly walked a few steps, and stopped again as Tessa tried to lead her away from the herd. Jodi squeezed her legs, made clicking sounds, and wiggled the lead rope to try and convince Scout to walk forward.

"I guess it'll just take some time to train her to be a good ridin' horse," Jodi said.

"She'll be a fine horse in no time," Tessa reassured her friend. "Especially if you ride with us so she can follow behind our horses."

Scout seemed uneasy with the attention she was receiving, especially after the other horses wandered off. Although she had been subjected to dominance and even aggression by the other horses, like all equines, Scout was a social animal and longed for the security of the other horses. The clearly established pecking order actually created harmony within the herd once each members' status was determined.

The girls concluded their visit by feeding Scout a generous portion of the donated feed. Scout remained on edge as she ate, even though she was not being threatened by the other horses.

"She's still a bit unsettled in this new pasture," Tessa observed.

Jodi pressed her cheek against the mare's furry neck and breathed in the warm, comforting equine smell. As she stroked the horse's buff-colored mane, she whispered, "I'll take you home with me real soon, and you'll have your very own pasture. You'll get stronger and healthier, and you won't be chased by other horses." Scout lifted her neck and snorted as she shook her head from side to side. "Gross!" Jodi exclaimed. "You just sprayed snot all over me."

Tessa laughed. "Don't take it personally, it happens to all of us."

When Scout finished her feed, the girls petted her one last time and departed on their bikes. "Do you want to go ridin' with me?" Tessa asked as they peddled their bicycles along the edge of Rocky Point Road. "You can ride Snuffy again."

"Thanks," she answered, "but I'm going home and put in the last five fence posts. Then all we'll have left is to stretch and nail up the wire, and then we're done."

Tessa shot her friend an admirable glance as she continued peddling her bike. "You're the most determined 13-year-old I've ever known."

"You'd do the same if you were this close to having your own horse, or rather, having your own horse in your own back yard."

Tessa nodded as she gripped the handlebars. She shifted to riding one-handed as she tucked a strand of golden hair behind her ear. She reflected to just a few years ago, when she was only 11-years-old and had assisted her daddy, or rather kept him company, while he built their horse fence and then the barn. And now she loved every day she rode her horse. Tessa was warmed with the thought that her newest friend would now experience that same special bond, the love of a horse that she and her other cowgirl friends had discovered.

## Chapter 11

When Jodi reached her house, she found her mom already home. "I forgot this was your half day at work," she said as she greeted her mom.

Mrs. Robertson smiled at her daughter, and then noticing her dirty arms and legs, asked, "Have you been riding horses this morning?"

Jodi did not wish to lie, but she did not want to reveal her secret either. "Yes ma'am, I was with Tessa, and we were playing with the horses."

Mrs. Robertson was delighted. "You sure have met a lot of nice girls. I'm amazed at how many new friends you've made in just the short time since we moved here."

"Yeah, you're right." Changing the subject, she added, "I'm going out back to dig more post holes. I need to get the last five dug, and then we can start putting up the wire."

"Come on sport," her mother gestured. "I'll help you dig the holes. Let's surprise your daddy and have them all done by the time he gets home tonight." She turned to Sam and winked. "Maybe your little brother will help us too."

Digging post holes was hard enough for any adolescent girl, but was especially challenging for a smaller-than-average, 13-year-old. But with help from her mom and younger brother, the trio dug the remaining five post holes. Sam held a carpenter's level on each post while Jodi pushed dirt into the gaps and her mom packed down the dirt.

After they had completed the task, Sam asked, "Can I go inside now?"

Mrs. Robertson smiled at her son whose clothes and skin were streaked with dirt. "Yes, Sam, you were a big help to us."

"Thanks, Sam," Jodi added.

Jodi stood near her mom, eyes cast down and shoulders sagging. The thought of Scout cantered into her mind. She knew she should be happy now that the hardest part of fence building was complete, but she was filled with despair. She dreaded telling her parents about her dun-colored, half-ton secret. She was so close to having her own horse right in her own back yard, but it could all fall apart if her parents wouldn't allow her to keep it. She took a deep breath and looked up at her mom.

"Momma, I need to ask you something. But I need you to say yes and convince Daddy to say yes too, or I don't know what I'll do."

Mrs. Robertson looked down at her daughter and saw that the determination Jodi had while digging the post holes had now turned to distress. "What is it dear?"

Jodi didn't know where to start. Tears welled up in her eyes, and her lip started to quiver.

"What's wrong sweetheart?" her mom repeated as she reached down and hugged her daughter. "You should be excited that we are building you a horse pasture. That means you'll be getting a horse soon."

"The problem is," Jodi hesitated as she took a deep breath. "I, uh, I already have a horse." She paused to wipe the tears that were now flowing freely down her face. She looked up at her

*Chapter 11*

mom and continued her story. "I was afraid to tell you and daddy because you might make me return her. But she's such a sweet horse, and the owner doesn't want her anymore. Tessa and the other girls have been helping me take care of her."

Her mom was dumbfounded. "You already have a horse?" She stepped back and looked down at her daughter. "Where in the world did you find a horse and how did you pay for it?"

"Actually," Jodi started to answer as she looked up at her mom. Tears spilled from her eyes and ran down her dirty cheeks. "Scout found us." Jodi described how they discovered the horse tangled in a rope and without any food or water, and how the man was going to turn it loose on the Prairie and let it fend for itself. "Kris offered the man $15 dollars and said that I needed a horse real bad and that I would take it off of his hands." Jodi wiped her eyes, which left another dirt-stained streak across her cheek. "I didn't know what to say. Next thing I knew I had agreed to pay the man within a week and I was leading the horse away."

"Where's the horse now?"

Jodi cast her eyes down as she answered. "She's in Mr. Taylor's pasture. My friends all gave me some grain so I can feed her every day, and they loaned me some tack and supplies until I get my own." She looked up and pleaded. "Momma, please tell me I can keep Scout. Scout needs me to take care of her, and I sure do need a horse."

Silence fell over the pair as her mom processed the story. Then Mrs. Robertson smiled, reached out her arms, and embraced Jodi as her young daughter sobbed.

"I'm sorry I kept this secret from you. I just didn't know what to do. And I am so scared that you and daddy won't let me keep her."

"Well, I can't speak for your dad, but we did agree to buy you a horse," her mom said as she caressed her daughter's back. "Let's see what he has to say when he gets home from work." Mrs. Robertson released her embrace and gazed down at her daughter's tear-streaked face. "Tell me, is this horse safe to ride or is it untrained and unruly?"

Jodi sniffed as she started to explain. "The horse used to be for a little girl to ride. I've sat on her back several times and walked around the pasture, and she didn't buck or run away with me. I think she'll be safe. Claire and the other cowgirls will help me train her."

Her mom held out her arms and once again hugged her daughter. "It sounds like you have the best support system you could ever hope for with all of your new friends. We'll talk to your daddy tonight and see what he has to say."

And with that, Jodi's mom received another big dirty hug from her brave 13-year-old daughter who had just muscled up enough strength to dig five post holes and enough courage to tell her mother about the secret named Scout.

"Well, it sounds to me like all we have to do is nail up the fence wire and pay the man $15 dollars, and we'll be done with this project," Jodi's father said after hearing the story about the rescued horse. "I wasn't planning to buy you a skinny, wormy, injured, and rejected horse, but if you think you can train her to be safe, then she's all yours. And," he added as he winked at his daughter, "I was planning to spend a little more than $15 dollars."

Jodi was ecstatic. She hugged both of her parents, not even bothering to rein in her happy sobs.

*Chapter 11*

Saturday morning was the final work day for building the new horse pasture. Tessa, Andi, and Kris came over to help finish the fence. Mr. Brown joined them. He knew that once Jodi got her horse, she would experience the same responsibilities, fulfillment, and companionship that his daughter and the others had with their horses.

With everyone's help, the new fence wire was stretched out around the perimeter of the new pasture, stapled to all the posts, and the entire project completed by mid-afternoon.

"Now can I go over and get Scout and bring her home?" Jodi pleaded as she looked up at her dad.

"Yes, I suppose you can now that the fence is finished," he replied. "But first, fill up a bucket with water so she'll have something to drink when she gets here."

"Come on," Kris gestured to Jodi. "We'll ride over with you. That way Scout can follow us on our horses, and she won't mind leaving the other horses behind."

Mr. Robertson turned to Mr. Brown and shook his hand. "I don't know how to thank you for all the work you've helped us with."

"Seeing that smile on your daughter's face is thanks enough for me," Mr. Brown replied.

About two hours later, Mrs. Robertson called out to her husband. "I hear the girls riding up now. Let's go out and meet our new horse."

"Yes," he smiled. "And let's see the most excited girl in Gainesville, the one who finally has her very own horse."

## Chapter 12

Tessa stood stone-faced as she held the telephone receiver to her ear and tried to process Kris's distressing message. Daisy, LeeAnne's chestnut mare, was down with colic. Tessa knew that when a horse was stricken with colic, its abdominal pains could be so severe that persistent rolling was the only way for a horse to try to relieve its pain. Unfortunately, rolling back and forth could make the condition fatal by potentially twisting the intestines.

"LeeAnne and I have been taking turns walkin' her ever since we found her down a few hours ago, but she keeps trying to lie down and roll," Kris explained. "LeeAnne's mighty upset, so I wondered if you could come over and help us?"

"Yes, of course," Tessa agreed. "Has she drank any water?"

"No, she won't drink," Kris replied.

"Have you called the vet?"

Kris paused a moment before answering. "The vet will cost money that my parents don't have. Besides, she's colicked before, and we walked her and kept her from rollin' until she got better."

"I'll be right over to help," Tessa offered.

The sun had already set when Tessa's mom drove her the few blocks north to Kris and LeeAnne's house.

"I'll probably stay here all night to help with Daisy," Tessa told her mom.

*Chapter 12*

"Please call me in the morning and give me an update," Mrs. Brown replied. "You know that I'll worry. And Tessa, you are very kind to help LeeAnne with her sick horse."

Kris greeted Tessa when she arrived and pointed down the street. "LeeAnne's over there leading Daisy. It's easier to walk along the road where there's a street light instead of in the dark pasture." Kris hesitated a moment as she pushed up her glasses. "I came inside to call Andi and Gina. They'll be here soon to help us. I decided not to call Jodi. No need to spoil her excitement since she finally got a horse."

Tessa noticed the worried look on her friend's face. "What would you like me to do?" Tessa asked.

"Maybe you can keep LeeAnne company. I'm not very good at cheering her up, especially since we argue a lot. She just loves Daisy, and she keeps cryin' when poor Daisy lies down and tries to roll."

Tessa found the youngest cowgirl four houses down, standing next to the sick chestnut and stroking the mare's rough coat. The horse stood motionless with her entire frame drooping like a withered plant. The nearby streetlight lit up the darkened sky enough for Tessa to see LeeAnne's red puffy eyes.

"I'm wettin' huh stand still as wong as she doesn't wie down and woll," LeeAnne said as she pushed back the ringlets that spiraled down her face. "Huh belwy must be huhtin' weal bad 'cause she keeps nudging it. I know I wouldn't wanna keep walking if I had a belwy ache."

Tessa walked over and gently rubbed the stricken patient's shaggy and sweat-stained neck. Without a bareback pad or rider covering her back, Tessa noticed the mare's sunken withers and protruding belly. Tessa wondered why Daisy wasn't as fit and conditioned as the other horses were. Tessa's eyes softened as she looked over at LeeAnne. "Would you like me to walk her for a spell so you can go inside and rest? You look tired."

"Ok," LeeAnne sniffed. "Wet's walk back to the house so I can get a dwink." LeeAnne handed the lead rope to Tessa, and Tessa urged the horse to follow. "Please don't wet huh wie down and woll," LeeAnne pleaded. "I suh don't want huh twistin' huh insides."

Tessa sat in one of the fold-up chairs that someone had placed in the sisters' front yard. She continued to hold Daisy's lead, not because the sickened horse might run off, but out of habit. She could have tossed the lead rope over the mare's back, or tied it to her halter, or unclipped it all together and the horse would not have moved.

Darkness had set in, and so had the mosquitoes. Gazing at the darkened outline of the sick horse made Tessa thankful that neither of her horses had colicked, at least not yet. She had heard that feeding a bran mash every week would help ward off colic. So every Sunday - bran mash Sundays as she called it – she fed her two horses a bucket full of water-soaked bran, infused with a generous dash of mineral oil, and sugar-coated with a sprinkling of sweet feed. Her horses gobbled it down without the slightest inclination that it kept their 100 feet of intestines free flowing. And of course, she dewormed her two horses twice a year to purge any parasites because wormy horses were more prone to colic.

Tessa's thoughts were interrupted when the horse buckled at the knees and dropped to the ground. Tessa jumped up and tugged on the lead rope. "Come on girl, get up, I can't let you lay down and roll. Get up, get up now."

Daisy ignored the girl's instructions and laid flat on her side and commenced to roll. Tessa pulled harder on the rope and instinctively made clicking sounds with her tongue, the

*Chapter 12*

universal command for a horse to move. The ailing horse was unfazed by the handler's commands and thrashed back and forth to try and ease her abdominal pains.

Kris heard the commotion and ran out of the house. She grabbed the stick that she had laid by the front door, sprinted over to the horse, and tapped the patient on the rear. "Get up girl! Get up now!"

LeeAnne followed close behind her older sister. "Get up Daisy! Qwit wolling!" she cried.

The sick horse acquiesced to the girls' commands and painfully rose to her feet. LeeAnne wrapped her arms around her horse's dirty neck while tears spilled onto her cheeks and down her neck. "I'm sowy Daisy, but we just can't wet you woll."

Two more cowgirls – Andi and Gina – arrived to lend their help. The five girls walked together along the grassy edge of the neighborhood road, slowly leading the ailing horse and discussing the patient's symptoms and speculating on possible causes. They decided to work in pairs so one girl could lead the horse slowly around the darkened and quiet neighborhood, and the other could coax the sick equine back to her feet if she tried to roll.

"It's almost ten o'clock," Andi announced in her take-charge voice. "Gina and I'll take this shift so y'all can take a break and get some rest. Come back out around midnight and take over for us." She looked at Kris and added in a softer tone, "One of us will come and wake you if anything changes and we need your help."

Andi and Gina spent the next couple of hours tending to Daisy and swatting at the pesky mosquitoes that interrupted the otherwise tranquil night. One girl sat in a fold-up chair that she carried from spot to spot, while the other rested on an old towel on the damp ground. As the night dragged on, Daisy showed less inclination to roll or to even move. She either stood motionlessly, head sagging from a lifeless body, or laying prostrate in the damp grass. The neighbor's dog seemed to have accepted the girls' unusual nocturnal activities and had quit barking. The quietness of the night surrounded the girls, allowing them to occasionally doze as they maintained their vigilance over the sick horse.

The pair was alerted to the shadowy movement of two approaching figures and soon recognized them as Tessa and Kris.

"How's poor Daisy doing?" Kris asked. "We came to relieve you."

Andi shook her head. "Not too good. She's real weak and she's not movin' very much."

Gina rubbed her eyes and yawned. "What time is it?"

"Almost one o'clock," Tessa answered.

As the group huddled around the stricken horse, Andi pointed to the woods on the other side of the street. "We've been watching the fireflies over there. See how they blink? They're flying all around the trees and bushes, but they won't come out into the clearin'."

Kris looked up at the vastness above her. "The sky has cleared up since earlier in the evenin'. The moon's come out, and I can see the Big Dipper."

"And there's the North Star," Tessa said as she pointed to a bright star that appeared isolated from the other constellations.

"I saw a shooting star a little while ago," Gina announced. "It lit up the sky over the Prairie."

"It would be a beautiful night for a moonlight ride," Andi yearned. "But first we gotta concentrate on gettin' poor Daisy better."

*Chapter 12*

Kris turned to her friends. "Tessa and I can take over now so you can go inside and rest. Momma put out some pillows and sheets in the living room. One of you can sleep on the couch and the other on a pad on the floor. She figured you'd be hungry so she left some food on the kitchen counter. There's milk and tea in the refrigerator, so help yourselves to the food and drinks."

"Is LeeAnne sleeping?" Gina asked.

"Yeah, she finally crashed, but she'll probably wake up soon and come out to check on Daisy," Kris answered.

The new shift, consisting of Kris and Tessa, administered their limited medical knowledge to the ailing equine. They gently coaxed her to a pail of water, but Daisy showed no interest in drinking. They let the patient lay down as long as she didn't roll, and they settled in next to her while she remained motionless. The night air was clear, but a light fog was starting to settle over the neighborhood.

"You know, I should be nicer to LeeAnne," Kris admitted as she stared straight ahead into the darkness. "But she can be such a pest, and I get so tired of her taggin' along with me every single day."

The two girls were continuing their conversation when they spotted a short, spindly figure with unruly curls emerge into view.

"How's my hohse doing?" LeeAnne asked as she rubbed her eyes. She hesitated and yawned. "Is she bettuh yet?" LeeAnne didn't wait for a reply as she shifted her eyes from the two girls to the infirmed horse. "She doesn't wook any bettuh. She wooks wike she still huhts."

Tessa wanted to sound encouraging, but the words just weren't there. "She's hangin' in there."

About that time another figure appeared from the darkness and walked toward the girls, a larger, stouter person wearing a baseball cap. He was slightly slumped over, and his hands were tucked into his front pants pockets. Kris and LeeAnne immediately recognized the person as their father.

"How's she doin'?" Mr. Kay asked.

"She's still colicky, and she's gotten weaker," Kris reported.

"Daddy, can we call the vet now?" LeeAnne pleaded. "She huhts weal bad, and she weally needs to be doctuhed."

The man shook his head. "As much as I hate to, I think we're gonna hafta' call him out," he replied. "You girls have done about all you can do." He directed his attention to his oldest daughter. "Kristin, it's almost three o'clock. Do you wanna call him now or wait until morning?"

LeeAnne started sobbing. "We need to call him now, daddy. Wook how bad she is."

"Ok," her dad agreed.

"I'll go to the house and call Dr. Anderson now," Kris offered as she walked away.

A long hour passed before the three girls – LeeAnne, Kris, and Tessa - spotted headlights slowly approaching. A large, white pickup truck pulled up, and a robust man wearing a cowboy hat and boots emerged from the truck. "Howdy," he said as he nodded at the girls. He looked over at the listless chestnut and added, "Looks like a sick one alright."

"We've been walking her since about five o'clock this afternoon when we found her down and rollin'," Kris reported. "We figured she had colic again. We were hoping not to call you out, especially in the middle of the night, but she's done gotten worse."

*Chapter 12*

LeeAnne sniffed and wiped her eyes. "Huh belly huhts weal bad. And she keeps weachin' awound and nudgin' huh side with huh nose."

Tessa turned to Kris. "I'll wake up Andi and Gina and let them know the vet's here. They'll probably want to come out and watch." She handed the cotton lead to LeeAnne and headed to the house.

"Can you point this at her?" Dr. Anderson asked as he handed a flashlight to Kris. He walked around to the patient's left side and placed a stethoscope against the horse's chest and listened to her beating heart. He checked his watch multiple times as he listened. The two sisters remained silent as the doctor concentrated. "Fifty, that's not good," he mumbled.

He placed the stethoscope against the patient's left flank, listened for abdominal sounds, repositioned it to a different spot, and listened again. Then he walked around to her right side and repeated the process. "I don't hear any gut sounds," the vet reported.

Dr. Anderson motioned to Kris. "Follow me over to the truck with the light." He walked over to the topper that covered the back portion of his truck, opened one of the many drawers, and pulled out a thermometer. "Let's see what her temperature is." Daisy barely flinched as the vet lifted her tail and inserted a thermometer into her rectum. "Here, can one of you girls hold her tail to the side?" he asked as he clipped a string to her tail.

"I'll do it," LeeAnne mumbled as she released her grip on the lead rope and walked around to Daisy's rear. Daisy was now without a handler, but she continued her lifeless stance with no threat of walking away. As LeeAnne held up Daisy's tail, she noticed the string attached to the thermometer.

Dr. Anderson walked to Daisy's front, and without looking over at Kris, said, "Point the flashlight at her mouth, will ya?"

With one hand on the halter, he reached over and lifted her top lip and examined her gums. "Her membranes are pale," he reported in a barely audible voice. With the tip of his finger, he pressed firmly onto the gums above her front teeth. "Dehydrated, I'm not surprised."

He walked back to her rear and removed the thermometer. "Shine the light over here," he instructed as he wiped the thermometer on a rag that he pulled from his back pocket.

"What's huh tempwuhtuah?" LeeAnne asked as she tried to hold back her sniffles.

"I'm afraid it's low, 95 degrees," he answered. "She's probably in shock."

About that time, Andi, Gina, and Tessa emerged from the darkness. Dr. Anderson nodded to the new arrivals. "Howdy," he said with no hint of geniality. He was focused on his infirmed patient. "She's a sick one alright."

The vet walked over to his truck while Kris followed with the flashlight. He retrieved a long plastic glove and inserted his right hand into the casing. He pulled the long plastic handle up and over his elbow. "I need to palpate her colon," he mumbled. Standing to the left of her tail and facing the horse's hip, he inserted his covered hand into her rectum. He extracted some feces and crumbled them between his plastic-wrapped fingers. "Dry and full of sand," he reported. "Has she defecated since you've been walking her?" he asked to no one in particular.

"No," Kris replied. "Not for us."

"And not during our shift either," Gina added.

Silently, he continued palpating the sick horse, pausing several times to remove the fecal material. The girls remained mute during the exam. After several long minutes, he extracted his arm, unrolled the glove, and turned toward Kris, the one holding the flashlight. "I'm terribly sorry to tell you this, but the

## Chapter 12

poor horse's gut is twisted. The only way to save her is to do emergency surgery. That's mighty expensive, and it may be too late. I'm sorry."

LeeAnne turned to Tessa and started sobbing. Tessa hugged her friend while she too started crying.

Kris's throat tightened when she heard the fatal diagnosis. "I'll go get my dad," she said as she handed Gina the flashlight and disappeared into the darkness.

"LeeAnne, let's you and me go to the house too," Tessa said warmly as she continued to wrap her arms and her heart around her young friend.

A few minutes later two figures, one carrying a flashlight, walked over to the truck where the vet was cleaning up. It was Kris and her father.

Dr. Anderson turned to Mr. Kay. "I'm terribly sorry. These girls did everything they could to try and save the horse, but the kindest thing we can do now is euthanize her so she's no longer suffering."

"I hate that," Mr. Kay replied. "But I guess that's what we'll hafta do."

"Burying a horse is no easy task," the vet said. "Do you know anyone with a backhoe who can dig a hole for you?"

Gina spoke up as she overheard the sad conversation. "I can ask some of the farmers on Crown Road if one of them has a backhoe."

"I'd appreciate it if you'd check around and find someone who could dig a hole for us," said Mr. Kay. "But it's too early right now. You should wait 'til morning."

"Where do you want to bury her?" Dr. Anderson asked. "It'll be easiest for y'all if I euthanize her right next to where you're going to dig the hole."

"I don't know." Mr. Kay turned to his daughter. "Come on Kristen, let's walk over to those woods and look around for a clearing."

Kris only nodded as she wiped away the tears that kept emerging from behind her glasses and clouding her vision. She trailed behind her dad as he shined the flashlight in search of Daisy's final resting spot.

After the two had walked away, Dr. Anderson turned to Andi, who was now holding the lead rope that was attached to Daisy's halter. "I don't understand why this horse looks so poor. She's skinny and her coat's thick and rough. She doesn't look healthy at all. I know you gals take good care of your horses, so I wonder why she's different. I want to check her teeth." He motioned to Gina and said, "here, shine the flashlight toward her mouth." He reached his index finger back past the bottom molars to the spot on the gum where her teeth ended. He pressed down on the mare's gum until she opened her mouth. "Humm," he said as he palpated her teeth. "I'm feeling some mighty sharp points," he reported. After completing the oral examination, he wiped his hand on his jeans and turned to Andi and Gina. "My guess is that these points are painful in her mouth when she tries to eat, which causes her to drop her food. Then she probably nudges around in the sand trying to eat the grain she's dropped. She's picking up both sand and parasites that way. Does she raise her head when she's being ridden?"

Andi nodded. "Yeah, come to think of it, she lifts her head and fights with the bit when LeeAnne rides her."

"I'm willing to bet that those teeth are the source of her problems – worms, colic, and rough riding. Her teeth needed floating to remove those rough points. But I'm afraid that won't help her now."

*Chapter 12*

Kris and her dad returned to where the vet, two girls, and sick horse were standing. "We found a clearing in the woods where we can bury poor Daisy," Mr. Kay announced sadly.

"Ok. Can you show these two gals the spot so they can lead her over there? I'll be right there."

Kris pressed her trembling lips together as she tried to maintain her composure. But she could no long hold back her tears. "I'm sorry, but I can't stay out here and watch. I'm going inside," she said as she turned for the house. Her sobs could be heard after she disappeared into the darkness.

Gina pulled on the horse's lead rope while Andi gently coaxed the mare from behind as they followed Mr. Kay to Daisy's final resting place. As hard as they tried, the two girls could not fight the tears that continued to well up. The sorrow of the situation was made worst by the horse almost refusing to walk to the site of her grave, not because she knew her fate but because she was too sick and weak to move.

When they finally reached the location, Mr. Kay said, "I'll take it from here. You gals go inside with the others."

Mrs. Kay was in the kitchen trying to comfort her two daughters when Andi and Gina walked into the house. The sadness that draped across their faces sent the two sisters awash in more tears.

Tessa turned to Mrs. Kay, "Can I take LeeAnne and Kris to my house? That might be easier than havin' them stay here right now. I can call my mom to come get us."

LeeAnne was too numb and emotional to respond. But Kris managed to collect herself. "I'll be ok," she sniffed. "I'll stay here and help bury Daisy."

Mrs. Kay turned to Tessa. "Yes, that would be kind of you to keep LeeAnne at your house for the day."

Andi looked over at Gina. "Let's go to my house, eat some breakfast, and then find someone with a backhoe."

"Ok," Gina replied. She walked over to Mrs. Kay and quietly said, "Please tell Mr. Kay we'll call as soon as we find someone with a backhoe."

It was eight thirty in the morning, and the sun was already heating up the morning air when the low rumbling of a tractor could be heard approaching the house. "I'll go outside," Mr. Kay told his wife.

"I'm coming too," Kris added.

The farmer introduced himself to Mr. Kay and said, "I'm sorry we have to meet under these circumstances. I understand you need a hole dug to bury your daughter's horse. I've come to dig it for you."

Kris and her father were standing near the clearing while the grave was being dug when Jodi rode up on her bike.

"Oh Kris, I'm so sorry about Daisy," Jodi said as she dropped her bicycle and ran over and hugged her friend. "I called to see if you and LeeAnne could go riding today and your mom told me what happened." She gasped as she glanced over at the corpse, feeling her stomach churn with the same sadness that was draped over the others.

As hard as Kris tried to fight it, Jodi's sentiment triggered another round of tears. Jodi continued to hug her grieving friend. "Come on. Let's go to my house. You can spend the day with me."

Kris walked over to her dad. "If you don't mind, I'm goin' with Jodi."

"That's fine, dear. We'll take care of the rest." He turned to Jodi. "Thank you for taking Kristen home with you. She's been up most of the night and she needs to rest."

*Chapter 12*

After the hole was dug and the deceased horse pushed into her grave, the farmer reversed the process and used the backhoe to push the dirt back into the hole. When the void was filled, he turned off his tractor and walked over to Mr. Kay. "I think that'll do it."

"You can't imagine how much we appreciate you coming over here so quickly and doing this. I don't think the girls could have coped with seeing their dead horse lying out here. How much do I owe you for your work?"

"You don't owe me a thing. I'm glad I could oblige. I was just being neighborly," he said as he offered his hand. Then the farmer climbed onto his tractor, started the engine, and motored back to his farm.

## Chapter 13

LeeAnne slumped over the kitchen table as she picked at the bowl of oatmeal that Tessa's mom had placed in front of her.

"Please try to eat some breakfast, dear," Mrs. Brown said as she tried to coax the visitor. "It will help you feel better."

LeeAnne attempted to smile and acknowledge the lady's kindness, but the broken-hearted girl had no smiles in her. "Thank you, I'll twy," she mumbled as she cast her eyes down at the bowl in front of her.

Tessa placed her hand on her grieving friend's shoulder and tried to encourage her. "You have a horse here to ride anytime you want. Snuffy can be your pony, and you can ride him every day until your parents buy you another horse."

LeeAnne whispered as she continued staring at her breakfast. "My pawents can't affuhd to get me anothuh hohse. And Kris won't shaeh Patches wiff me. She's mean and bossy."

"Well Snuffy'll be your new horse," Tessa assured her. "For as long as you want, he's yours to ride."

LeeAnne initially resisted her friends' invitations to ride. And she ignored her sister's urging as well. But LeeAnne soon realized that spending her summer days alone, grieving over Daisy while her parents worked and her sister and the other cowgirls went riding, was far worse than riding a replacement horse. LeeAnne soon began riding Tessa's pony and joining the other cowgirls on some of their outings.

*Chapter 13*

Tessa told her, "Just call and I'll have Snuffy groomed and ready for you to ride." Tessa hoped that LeeAnne's giddy and silly personality would soon return to the youngest cowgirl in the Idylwild clan. But so far, only sadness prevailed.

One morning, just over a week after Daisy had died, LeeAnne called Tessa to say she was on her way over to ride. "Kris and Andi awh helping Jodi with huh new hohse, but I don't want to wide with them," LeeAnne said.

"Let's just the two of us ride today," Tessa offered. "And we'll go someplace new."

The pair ambled down the driveway, and when they reached Crown Road, they turned right and headed west instead of their typical eastward direction. With no destination in mind, they continued along the oak-covered dirt road. LeeAnne remained quiet and somber, and the only sounds that followed the pair were an occasional wren or chickadee voicing its presence.

Several minutes into the ride, LeeAnne broke the girls' silence. "I'm still so sad," she admitted as she glanced over at her friend, "especially when I wook at the backyauhd and see that Daisy's not theuh. Wast night, I told my mom that I wanted to go somewheuh else."

Tessa studied her still grieving friend. "What did she say?"

"She suggested that I visit Aunt Wita and Uncle Jack and my two younguh cousins in Tampa."

"What a good idea," Tessa nodded. "When are you goin' to Tampa?"

LeeAnne rolled her shoulders. "I don't know. Momma's gonna call Aunt Wita tonight."

The girls continued their stroll along the tranquil dirt road, and when they reached the paved street, they directed their horses right, along the grassy edge of Rocky Point Road.

Tessa pointed to a clearing. "Hey, look, they mowed around the ponds next to the Farm Bureau building. I've never ridden over there before. Let's check it out."

The two girls crossed the paved road and reined their mounts toward a series of lagoons that were nestled beyond a stand of pine trees. LeeAnne led the way on the brisk-walking pony, who was out-striding Tessa's lazy palomino.

LeeAnne looked back at her friend from the lead position and asked, "Why do you suppose he's cawed Speedy? There's nothing fast about him."

Tessa shrugged. "I don't know. Maybe it was just wishful thinking."

LeeAnne managed a half-hearted smile. "Well, it shuh didn't wouk."

"No, it backfired," Tessa laughed as she brushed back some golden strands of hair and tucked them behind her ear. "He's slow as molasses." Tessa had to holler up to LeeAnne who had moved further ahead on the fast-paced pony. "I've lived here all my life, and I've never seen these ponds, not until someone finally cleared and mowed around 'em!"

LeeAnne and the energetic pony rounded a corner and almost stumbled over a large dark object that was resting on the ground. Shaded from the mid-morning sun was an alligator lying next to the shrubs that lined one of the basins. Startled from the unexpected pony, the gator rose on its front feet, opened its massive jaws, and hissed. The pony's prey instinct kicked in and instantly, he spun around and bolted. LeeAnne screamed, and as the pony ran past Tessa, LeeAnne lost her balance and fell to the ground. Snuffy galloped away.

LeeAnne jumped to her feet, and like the scared pony, ran away from the frightening gator.

*Chapter 13*

"What happened?" Tessa hollered. "What spooked Snuffy?"

LeeAnne stopped running when she realized she wasn't being pursued by the gator. "Theuh's a gigantic gatuh ovuh theuh, and Snuffy almost stepped on it," she cried as she pointed to the pond. "It opened its mouth and wouhed!" Tears rolled down LeeAnne's face, and she began to shake.

Tessa jumped down from her horse and put her arms around her young friend. "Are you hurt?"

"I don't think so," LeeAnne said as she sniffed and wiped the tears that emerged from her eyes. She looked around for her mount. "Wheuh did Snuffy go?"

"I don't know. We'll find him. But first, let's make sure you're ok," Tessa said as she tried to calm her friend.

LeeAnne was unable to control her tears. She was still so emotionally fragile after having buried her beloved Daisy just last week. And now, falling off Snuffy next to a threatening gator had the youngest cowgirl completely shaken up. Tessa hugged her distraught friend while LeeAnne wept.

"What if Snuffy's wun away and we can't find him?" she cried. "I'll have caused you to wose youh hohse too."

Tessa tried to console her friend. "It's ok. Snuffy knows the way home. He'll probably be waiting for us at the barn."

"What if he gets hit by a cauh when he wuns acwoss the woad?" LeeAnne sobbed.

"Don't you worry, we'll find him, and he'll be just fine." Tessa hoped she was right about her pony. "Hop on Speedy and we'll look for him."

They rode double along the mowed trail back to the street. They crossed Rocky Point Road and headed south until they reached Crown Road. They traveled east, and comforted by the thick shade of the majestic oaks, they followed the dirt road to

Tessa's driveway. When they turned into the drive, they were greeted by a joyful whinny.

"Snuffy!" LeeAnne cried. "I'm so glad you'a heuh!" LeeAnne slid off the tall palomino and hurried over to the pony. "Oh, no, he's done bwoke the weins. He must'a stepped on 'em when he wan off."

"Don't worry about the reins," Tessa assured her friend. "He's home, and neither of you are hurt. That's all that matters." Tessa breathed a double sigh of relief, for her friend and her pony, both who were safely back.

## Chapter 14

Kris held the telephone receiver to her ear as Mrs. West, a long-time resident of the Idylwild neighborhood, explained the developer's plans. "Mr. Moody wants to develop his 50 acres by building a subdivision with about 45 houses on it," Mrs. West said. "He is lobbying the commissioners saying the dirt road doesn't meet county specifications. Since the county wants the additional tax revenue that his development would provide, they are considering widening and paving Crown Road."

"That would be terrible," Kris exclaimed. "What can we do to save our road?"

"I called the local newspaper, the *Gainesville Sun*, and explained our problem. I asked them to write an article about our rural neighborhood and our lovely dirt road. A newspaper reporter is coming out tomorrow. If you and your friends show up on your horses, you could be included in the story."

"I'll round up as many girls as I can," Kris assured her. "Where should we meet you and what time?"

"Ten o'clock tomorrow morning in my driveway," Mrs. West replied.

"We'll be there."

The next morning, Kris snuck out to the back yard to ride Patches. She was extra careful to not let LeeAnne know her intentions to take the pony. This was no ordinary morning. Her mom had told her to share Patches with LeeAnne, at least for the next week until LeeAnne went to Tampa to visit their aunt and uncle. And today was LeeAnne's designated day to ride the pinto. But Kris couldn't relinquish the pony on such an important day, even if her kid sister was still grieving over the loss of Daisy. Kris's only recourse was to slip off with Patches before LeeAnne came outside. She knew she would be in trouble when her parents found out, but she was willing to risk their wrath, even if it meant being grounded from riding for a few days.

Kris swung onto Patches, reined her around, and kicked the pony into a fast trot. She was departing their front yard when LeeAnne ran out of the house yelling at Kris to stop. Kris continued her hurried pace, trotting through her neighbor's front yard and not even slowing down when she crossed the paved road.

When she reached the woods trail, Kris cued Patches into a canter. As they rounded a bend in the trail, Kris spotted a snake just a few strides in front of her and her cantering pony. Her momentary view of the reptile was sufficient to mentally identify the serpent. *Rattlesnake!* Kris screamed. Patches started to hesitate as Kris fiddled with the reins, but she kicked her pony hard. The pinto must have sensed the danger lying in her path because she leaped over the snake like it was a 3-foot high log.

Kris had no time to prepare for the pony's enormous jump and was lurched forward. Instinctively, she grabbed hold of the horse's mane and gripped with her legs, a response that prevented her from falling off. But during the jump, Kris's face crashed against her mount's upward arching neck, sending her glasses flying into the air. Kris reined Patches to a halt. Her nose and lip immediately began to throb. She held her hand to her

*Chapter 14*

face and rested her forehead on the pony's crest. She closed her eyes and tried to calm her racing heart. After a few moments, she sat up and noticed blood in her hand. Her lip was split and worse, her glasses were missing.

Kris was the most solution-oriented of the Idylwild Cowgirls, and now she needed an immediate solution to an unanticipated problem. She removed the bandana that restrained her unruly hair and held it tight against her upper lip. The makeshift compress eventually stopped the flow of blood. She slid off her horse and tried to find her missing glasses, but with her uncorrected eyesight, she couldn't focus on the ground around her. She abandoned the search in hopes that her friends would ride back over here after the newspaper interview and help her find the lost glasses. Now she would have to rely on her sense of direction and Patches' eyesight to navigate to the meeting site with the reporters.

Her close encounter with the poisonous snake, the sharp blow to her face, and now her inability to focus had this normally fearless equestrian shaken and unsettled. The guilt of taking Patches when she knew it was LeeAnne's designated day to ride, just added to her uneasiness. She tried to compose herself as she nudged Patches toward the dirt road. She was needed at a very important gathering to discuss a grave topic – preservation of Crown Road.

As she rode along the path, Kris wondered if a black cloud was following her and her sister. First, Daisy died. Then LeeAnne almost tripped over an alligator and was thrown from Snuffy. Now Kris's vision was gone, and she didn't know how long it would be before she could see again, either with her old glasses, which would be a miracle if they were still intact or with a new pair. She would surely be grounded, twice grounded, once for taking Patches and another for carelessly losing her expensive glasses. And the storm was still building, threatening to destroy the rural nature of their entire Idylwild neighborhood if Mr. Moody succeeded in paving Crown Road.

Mrs. West stood in the dirt road, shielded from the sun by the massive branches of a heritage live oak, as she was being interviewed by a female reporter from the *Gainesville Sun*. Another reporter was photographing the picturesque road and its giant trees. The interview abruptly stopped when the three adults spotted the equestrians approaching from both directions. Mrs. West smiled. She had not revealed to the newspaper staff that they would be joined by the Idylwild Cowgirls.

The equestrians gathered at Mrs. West's driveway. Included in the crowd was LeeAnne, aboard Tessa's pony. LeeAnne and Kris briefly locked eyes, and when they did, LeeAnne scowled and stuck her tongue out at her older sister. "Suhves you wight," she hissed when she saw her sister's cut lip and missing glasses.

After a few tense moments, Andi broke the silence. "We love this dirt road, and we ride on it almost every day, and we don't want it paved or these beautiful trees cut down."

Kris held her hand in front of her mouth and tried to conceal her injury as she pretended to focus on the newspaper reporter. "None of us want this road disturbed. It's the shadiest place to ride in the summer."

"Sometimes, we ride our horses on the dirt road at night," Tessa added. "We tell ghost stories and pretend there are goblins lurking behind the big oak trees."

"If the woad is paved, then cauhs will dwive fast," LeeAnne squeaked. "They might wun ovuh us."

When it was her turn to speak, Jodi locked eyes with the reporter and said with such intensity that the other cowgirls shuddered at the gravity of the situation. "This road deserves a

*Chapter 14*

special designation, like *Scenic Road,* that will protect it forever and ever."

Mrs. West smiled as she glanced around at the cowgirls. Then she nodded at the reporter. "These young ladies have expressed many of the concerns that are shared by the other residents in the Idylwild neighborhood. As you can see, this is a beautiful piece of the countryside. Even though the price of our land might be higher with a paved road, that won't compare to the value we place on our lovely rural landscape and this scenic dirt road that connects us to each other and to Gainesville."

"You girls are very dedicated to protecting your neighborhood and this special road," the newspaper reporter said as she folded up her notebook and tucked it into her pack. "We appreciate you talking to us, and we'll include many of your comments in the article, especially," she emphasized as she looked over at Jodi, "your suggestion to make this dirt road a Scenic Road. Can we take your picture for the newspaper?"

As the group was disbanding, Toby, one of the motorbike riders, arrived in a black pickup truck that was being driven by another young man. Tension still existed between Andi and the motorbike riders.

"Are you going to get to keep your dirt road?" Toby called out from the passenger's side of the truck.

"Don't know," Andi shrugged.

Toby took notice of the group that was dispersing, "That was quite a crowd that showed up."

"Yep. And they're gonna' write an article for the newspaper," Andi boasted.

"You wanna' race again?"

Andi shot him a look of confusion. "What do you mean?"

"You think your horse is so fast, see if he can beat this pickup."

"No way. I'm not foolish enough to think Bingo can outrun a truck." Andi turned her attention to the Ford with scratches on its side and a dent in the door just below the window where the driver rested his arm. "That truck looks pretty darn fast, at least faster than my horse. I would love to know how fast ole Bingo can run. Would you clock us if I raced him next to your truck?"

"Where, on this skinny dirt road?" Toby asked.

"Sure," Andi replied. "It's plenty wide enough for your truck, and me and Bingo don't take up much room. We'll gallop next to you if you don't cut us off."

"Sure, we'll do it," the driver agreed. He shifted the truck into first gear and released the clutch. Andi signaled Bingo to trot next to the moving vehicle. The road was so narrow that Andi could easily reach over and touch the truck's side mirror.

Andi raised her voice so she could be heard over the sound of the engine and pounding hooves. "I'm speedin' up so stay next to me!"

The driver hollered out his window. "Twenty-five miles per hour!"

Andi kicked her horse. "Faster Bingo, I know you can run faster!" Bingo accelerated again and was now running at breakneck speed. Andi's fluid body glided in unison with every long reaching stride.

"Thirty miles an hour! You're going 30 miles an hour!" the driver shouted.

*Chapter 14*

"Let me see!" Andi yelled back. And while maintaining her two-point jockey position, and Bingo sprinting at his top speed, Andi shifted her view and searched the dash for the gage that revealed Bingo's racing speed. "I see the speedometer! We ARE going 30 miles an hour!" She slowly shifted her weight back to an upright position and retreated her arms until her hands floated just above Bingo's withers. Those subtle cues were all that were needed to communicate to her mount. The Appaloosa responded instantly by slowing his pace to a bouncy trot followed by a brisk walk. "Good boy, Bingo, Good boy!" Andi shouted as she slapped his sweaty neck. "I can't believe you ran 30 miles an hour!"

Andi returned to her friends, and as she trotted up to the girls with a grin that stretched from one sun-fired cheek to the other, they wondered what bold, adventure-seeking stunt she would think of next.

"Thirty miles an hour!" Andi boasted as she again slapped the sweat-covered muscles that protruded from Bingo's neck. "He ran 30 miles an hour!"

After the excitement had subsided, Tessa turned to Andi. "We need to help Kris find her glasses. She lost 'em on the trail."

Andi squinted at her long-time friend. "You can't see much without those glasses, can you?"

Kris shook her head. The missing glasses were only part of her problem. Her lip throbbed, and she probably had dried blood streaked on her face. And how long, she wondered, would she be grounded from her horse and from riding with her friends?

"How did you make it over here if you can't see?" Andi asked.

"It wasn't much different than ridin' at night. I just relied on Patches."

"I don't want to help Kwis find huh glasses," LeeAnne barked. "She took Patches when it was my tuhn to wide huh. Sehves huh wight to wose huh glasses and bust huh wip."

With LeeAnne reluctantly following, the friends ambled along Crown Road taking their time while Andi broadcasted her race with the truck. As she recounted the relay, she gestured wildly in her characteristic Andi-style animation. Kris, on the

*Chapter 14*

other hand, was subdued and shrugged off sharing any details of her snake encounter. It wasn't even noon yet, and collectively the girls had already experienced more excitement than they could have anticipated.

When they reached the trail, they queued in single file, with Andi leading the procession, Kris following behind the leader, and LeeAnne trailing the pack.

"How much further until we start looking?" Andi called back to Kris.

"Not too much further," Kris answered. Although she couldn't see exactly where she was, Kris was relying on instinct and her ingrained knowledge of a trail that she had traversed so many times before.

"I hope it's not near where the sinkhole opened up!" Tessa shouted from her middle position in the pack.

"Watch out for the rattlesnake," Jodi called out. "It could be hiding anywhere."

The girls continued to scan left and right for the missing glasses. When they were almost at the end of the trail, Kris halted her pony. "We've gone too far," she almost whispered as she cast her eyes to the ground. "We've passed where I lost the glasses."

"Well let's turn around and try again!" Andi bubbled. The equestrians reversed direction, and this time, LeeAnne was in front. LeeAnne could never remember being the leader of the cowgirls. She was always a follower, usually pushed to the rear by her bossy sister or inadvertently ignored by the older girls. As the new leader, LeeAnne lifted her shoulders and her spirits, motioned the search party forward, and searched in earnest for her sister's lost glasses.

"I see 'em!" LeeAnne shouted as she rounded a bend in the trail. She slid off the pony and reached for the glasses that laid partially concealed under some bushes. "Hey, they ain't even bwoken!" she shouted again.

When she heard LeeAnne's announcement, Kris skirted around the two cowgirls that separated her from her kid sister. "Thanks, little sis, for finding my glasses," Kris said as she slid down from the pinto. "I'm really sorry for taking Patches today. I really am." And then she handed her sister the leather reins. "Here, you take Patches. You deserve her. She's yours for the rest of the week." The two sisters swapped mounts, and LeeAnne swung onto Patches' back. She sat tall and proud on her sister's horse with a grin that the others hadn't seen since the passing of her beloved Daisy.

The title of the article in the next day's paper read "*Idylwild Cowgirls Oppose Rural Road Development.*" The newspaper story described the neighbors' desires to protect their scenic dirt road and the century-old live oaks. The article then described Mr. Moody's plans to develop his parcel, and in the process, destroy the picturesque road. The story concluded with Jodi's question, *"Isn't there some kind of protection that could be placed on this road, like Scenic Road, that will protect it forever?"* Below the article was a large photograph of Mrs. West and the five cowgirls who had spoken out in opposition to the road development plan.

"Well, look at that!" Mr. Robertson exclaimed to his wife as he sat down for a quick breakfast and to glimpse the morning paper before he hurried off to work. "Jodi just got herself a new horse, and now she and her friends are on the front page of the newspaper!" He looked down the hallway and called out. "Jodi, come see your picture in the paper!"

Jodi ran to the kitchen followed closely by her younger brother. "Wow," she exclaimed. "There's my friends."

*Chapter 14*

"Let me read the article real quick so I can leave for work," Mr. Robertson said. "Then you can take your time and read it."

After breakfast was over and Jodi had described the interview with the newspaper reporter and photographer, she turned to her mother and said, "Scout's ankle has healed from the rope burn she got when she was tied up to the tree on the day we rescued her. Claire offered to help me train Scout. I think we're ready for some riding lessons."

"Hum," her mother considered. "What makes Claire qualified to teach you?"

Jodi explained that Claire's been taking weekly riding lessons from a horse trainer. "When we were all riding together a few weeks ago, Claire showed us what she has been teaching Shotsie. It's not like her horse will do tricks or anything, he's just so quiet and willing and easy to ride." She paused a moment as she looked up at her mother. "That's how I want Scout to be."

"Riding lessons," her mother considered again. "Maybe it is time for riding lessons."

## Chapter 15

With her parent's permission to start riding lessons, Jodi arranged to ride her horse to Claire's house and stay a few days so Claire could help her train Scout. But Jodi was not confident enough to attempt the three-mile ride alone along Highway 441 and across the vast Prairie to Claire's parent's farm. So she asked her friends to accompany her part way to meet Claire.

The next morning, Andi, Kris, and Tessa joined Jodi, and together the four cowgirls set their sights south toward the level green plain of Paynes Prairie. The morning was clear and the temperature rapidly rising when they started their ride. There was no sign of moisture on the plants even though a thunderstorm had drenched their neighborhood the previous afternoon. The heating and drying power of Florida's mid-morning, summer sun was in full force.

Cars were few and the road right-of-way recently mowed, so the girls did not fear either the passing vehicles or hiding reptiles. As they descended onto the Prairie, they were oblivious to the sounds that surrounded them. Birds that were not apparent to the casual eye were spewing forth multitudes of territorial songs. An imperceptible rustling in the grass along the mowed edge signified a large water turtle that was likely searching for a suitable spot to bury her eggs.

Movement in the weeds up ahead alerted the girls to a rabbit that was sniffing the daisy fleabane and pennywort and other

## Chapter 15

roadside plants. As the girls focused on the cottontail, a flock of blackbirds erupted from the willows nearby and startled the horses. Scout, who was green in her training and the least trail-worthy of the group, panicked and bolted forward into an uncontrollable gallop.

"Whoa! Whoa!" Jodi cried as she tried to stop her runaway horse. "Whoa!"

Just like Scout, horses have evolved for thousands of years to flee from danger. Their lightning-fast instinct to spin, bolt, and gallop has ensured the survival of these herd-bound mammals. Scout was following her primordial instinct to escape the frightening explosion of what could have been a deadly predator.

"Quick, let's catch her!" Andi shouted. "We have to stop her before she runs across the highway!"

The three girls kicked their horses into a gallop and chased after the runaway horse. "Turn her head left so she doesn't run into the road!" Kris called out to Jodi.

Andi broke from the group and galloped after the panicked horse. With her seat glued to the bareback pad, legs fastened around the barrel, and arms stroking back and forth in synchrony with each lengthening stride, the horse and rider appeared as one and the same. As Andi approached the fleeing horse, she yelled, "I'm comin' up on your right, and I'm gonna pull in front so I can stop you!" She reined Bingo left into the path of the panicked pair. "Whoa!" Andi commanded as she pulled back on the leather reins. "Whoa, now!"

Both horses gradually slowed to a bouncy trot and then to a choppy walk. Tessa and Kris caught up with the pair just as the panicked flight of the runaway horse had ended.

"Way to go, Andi!" Kris shouted. "That was some fancy ridin'."

Andi grinned and patted her mount's sweaty neck. "That was nothin' for Bingo, he loves racing other horses. And he especially likes to be in front. The problem was gettin' him to cut in front of Scout and make her stop." She turned to Jodi. "You were the big hero for hangin' on and keepin' Scout from runnin' into the road."

Scout's nostrils were flared, and the young mare heaved back and forth as she sucked for air. Jodi gasped as she too tried to catch her breath. "It happened so fast, I didn't know what to do. I was trying to hang on with my legs, but I think I was kicking her accidentally."

"Jodi, you did great to hang on and not fall off," Tessa reassured her.

Kris nodded in agreement. "The more you ride her, the more she'll get used to unexpected things, and the less she'll panic like that."

"Yep," Andi joked. "Come October, she'll be ready for the homecoming parade."

"The parade?" Jodi questioned, still winded and unsettled from the frightening experience.

"Yeah," Tessa replied, trying to restore Jodi's confidence.

"You mean with the floats and marching bands and all the people that line the road?" Jodi asked.

"That's it," Kris nodded. "They let horses in the parade, so we're gonna ride in it this year."

"Yep," Andi confirmed. "Come fall, our horses will be fancy parade horses."

The riders spotted two horses up ahead. The tallest, a chestnut with a white blaze that wrapped clear across its face, appeared like a spotlight a mile away. The accompanying horse was as rotund as a draft horse but only half the height of its bald-faced partner.

## Chapter 15

"Hey look, there's Claire! And that must be her little sister with her," Tessa announced.

Kris squinted as she gazed through her thick-rimmed glasses. "Looks like there's a dog following 'em." Kris was grateful that her eyesight was restored and that her kid sister didn't rat on her for taking Patches when it was LeeAnne's turn to ride. Otherwise, she would surely still be grounded and missing out on this journey.

The group broke into a trot until they closed the gap and met up with the two advancing riders.

"Howdy!" Claire called out as the two groups converged. "This is my sister, Mary Kate, and her horse King," she said as she gestured over to her riding partner.

Mary Kate grinned and waved to the Idylwild Cowgirls. She was only nine and still in elementary school, but she straddled her broad-backed horse with the same confidence as the older cowgirls. King, her mount, was predominately white but wore a swath of brown across his neck and face. He was handsome, perhaps even regal, which may have accounted for his royal name. The gelding was short, but where he lacked in height, he more than made up with a thick, broad girth. He looked to be as comfortable as the softest armchair and as calm as an old Bassett that slept next to the chair.

Claire hadn't expected to meet up with her friends so quickly. "Y'all made good time coming across the Prairie."

"We had some excitement along the way," Andi boasted as she glanced over at Jodi. This leader of the cowgirl clan craved excitement and adventure.

Jodi recounted Scout's panic and Andi's heroic rescue.

"So that's why Scout's so sweaty," Claire observed. "She's not used to galloping like that."

Movement off to her left caught Tessa's attention, and she noticed birds flying back and forth between a long strand of shrubs and the vast Prairie. "Is that the bird rookery you told us about last time we rode together?" Tessa asked Claire.

"Yep," Claire replied. "That's it all right. Pretty cool, huh?"

The girls nodded and then shifted their eyes to the lanky black and white spotted dog that stood obediently in the morning shade cast by the two horses. "What a pretty dog!" Jodi exclaimed.

"Thanks," Claire replied. "His name's Duke, and he loves to follow us."

"What kind of dog is he?" Kris asked.

"An English setter," Claire answered. "He was given to us by my parents' friends. Their back yard was too small, and he needed a place to run."

"He took up with Claire and me and he follows us on our horses," Mary Kate explained.

Jodi was concerned. "Aren't you worried he might get hit by a car?"

Claire nodded. "Yeah, but I'm teaching him dog obedience, so he'll listen to me when we're out riding."

"How do you know how to teach dog obedience?" Jodi asked.

"I didn't," Claire replied, "until my mom signed us up for a class and we've been attending every week."

Mary Kate couldn't resist ribbing her older sister. "Dad said he hopes Claire learns as much obedience as Duke does." The cowgirls laughed, knowing that their parents too would like more obedience infused into them.

"What are you teaching Duke?" Kris asked.

"Just the basics - sit, stay, heel, and come," Claire replied. "First I taught him those while on a leash," she explained. "Now

## Chapter 15

I'm teaching him those same commands from up on the horse. Let's see if he will obey with all of you around." Claire shifted in her saddle until she could see her dog. She pointed to Duke and commanded attention. "Duke, Duke, sit." The dog perked up his ears and stared back at Claire. "Duke, sit," she repeated. The dog hesitantly sat when he heard the order a second time. Claire held up her hand and instructed, "Duke, stay." Claire shifted her attention to the riders. "Let's walk toward my house. No one look at the dog or say anything to him."

The girls nudged their horses south, and when they had advanced about 30 feet, Claire turned back to the obedient dog and called out, "Duke, come!"

On command, Duke exploded toward the pack of horses, which sent Scout into another temporary panic. Jodi reined in her frightened horse before Scout could run off.

Claire apologized. "Oh, Jodi, I'm so sorry. I shouldn't have done that."

"It's ok," Jodi replied as she tried to calm her fidgety horse. "Scout needs to learn not to panic. Maybe you can train Duke while we're riding together and then Scout will learn not to spook so often."

"Yeah," Claire nodded. "That can be one of our horse training exercises over the next few days."

The girls proceeded south, absorbed in their multiple conversations while the setter trailed close behind.

Andi pointed left toward the middle of the expansive marsh. "Gina told me about a raised dike out there that crosses the middle of the Prairie." Andi lifted her shoulders and grinned at the group. "I think we ought'a ride the dike all the way back across the Prairie."

Tessa shook her head hesitantly as she looked out at the sea of marsh plants. "I don't know about that. Isn't there a fence on the other side? How would we get out?"

Andi reassured her. "Gina found an unlocked gate on the north side, so there's no problem gettin' out."

Kris wasn't convinced either, and she too hesitated at her friend's suggestion. "What if the dike's not high enough and we have to wade through the water?" she asked as she straddled her short-legged pony and dangled her legs only a foot above the ground. "I don't wanna ride where there's snakes and gators."

Tessa looked down at her pony and wished that today she had ridden her bomb-proof palomino. "Snuffy's afraid of alligators. I don't want him spooking from a gator and dumping me on the ground like he did LeeAnne, especially in the middle of the Prairie."

"Let's try it," Andi persisted. "If the dike's too low or full of weeds or there's too many gators, then we'll turn back," she reassured her two friends.

The group ascended the escarpment that marked the abrupt transition from the low Prairie to the higher uplands. Further ahead, they spotted a sign on the fence that read, *Paynes Prairie Preserve State Park.* A smaller sign proclaimed, *Future site of the Bolen Bluff Trail.*

Andi noticed a gap in the fence near the two signs and bubbled out her discovery. "That's it. There's how we reach the dike!"

Claire shook her head as she looked over at the exuberant leader. "That's a cattle gap. You can't ride across it. Your horse could break its leg."

Tessa wrinkled her brow as she looked at the contraption that was built specifically to keep livestock from crossing. "I'm not ridin' my pony across that."

*Chapter 15*

Andi grinned at the group with a look of mischievousness that the others should have recognized. "It'll be ok. Gina told me she found sound boards next to the fence where they put up the new sign. We'll use those boards to walk across."

"I don't know," Tessa cautioned, knowing it would be hard to convince her determined friend otherwise. "That'll be like walkin' a tightrope."

Andi wasn't giving up. "Our horses'll do it. Just watch." She slid off her mount and handed the reins to Kris. "Here, hold Bingo while I look for some boards." Andi scouted the fence line until she found two 2 x 4s, both about three feet long, that were partially covered by leaves and forest debris. "There's the boards Gina used to cross the cattle gap." When she reached down to grab the boards, large ants scurried in all directions. She banged the two boards together and tossed them to the ground. "There, that should get rid of the ants."

"What are you supposin' to do with the boards?" Kris asked.

Andi shot her friend a smirky grin. "You'll see." The leader carried the boards over to the cattle gap and dropped the planks perpendicular across the middle of the metal rails that formed the subterranean structure.

Tessa shook her head. "That ain't gonna work. The boards don't even reach from one side to the other."

Kris echoed her friend's concern for the plan that was unfolding in front of them. "One misstep on either side of the boards and our horses could fall through the holes and break their leg."

Andi surveyed the alignment of the wood that she had placed across the center of the cattle gap. "You're right, Tessa. I'll move the boards over to the edge." She repositioned the timbers so they rested on the right-hand side of the cattle gap. "That should work." Andi retrieved the reins from her friend and led her mount toward the improvised cattle gap crossing. Bingo halted when he saw the crisscrossing boards and poles. Andi tugged on the reins and clicked with her tongue until the horse acquiesced to his handler's commands. The boards began to slide as the horse's right front leg contacted the wooden planks, and when the boards shifted, he leaped, almost from a standstill, all the way across the earthen contraption.

"Good boy, Bingo!" Andi said as she petted his neck. "You're such a good horse!" Then she directed her attention to Kris and Tessa. "If big ole Bingo can get across those narrow boards then your ponies can too."

Kris took a deep breath. "Ok, I'll go next. But I'm gonna ride Patches across." The pinto, being an undersized horse of only 14 hands, and equally diminutive in width, was a full eight inches shorter and proportionally more narrow than Bingo. Although size was in her favor, Patches was a less cooperative mount, and when Kris nudged her to step onto the narrow wooden planks, the horse planted her feet and refused to budge. Kris squeezed her heels, clucked, and even flicked the reins back and popped the leathers onto the pony's rear. Patches stubbornly resisted her rider's cues and began to back up.

Kris called out to her friend who was reluctantly waiting her turn. "Tessa, ride Snuffy right behind Patches and push her with your horse while I kick."

"Sure," Tessa agreed. Tessa nudged her pony forward until Snuffy was on the heels of Patches. Now Tessa was coaxing the obstinate horse from behind while Kris cued her mount. The pinto finally reached out her delicate hooves and gingerly tiptoed across the wooden planks.

"Way to go Patches!" Kris exclaimed as she patted her mount's bicolored neck. "Good girl!"

*Chapter 15*

Tessa continued nudging her chestnut pony until her mount followed the horse in front, right across the wooden bridge that so dangerously straddled the moat below.

"We all made it across!" Andi exclaimed.

Kris didn't quite share the leader's enthusiasm. "Yeah, let's just hope we can make it all the way across the Prairie and not have to come back this way. That wasn't easy."

# Chapter 16

Andi, Kris, and Tessa waved goodbye to the other three riders – Jodi, Claire, and Mary Kate - and followed the dirt road east through an upland hammock of live oaks, cabbage palms, and sweetgums. The riders were mesmerized by the forest and its sharp contrast to the low-lying Prairie they had just crossed along the edge of the highway in the blazing sun. The woods were cooler, shadier, and melodic with songs of cardinals and wrens and vireos.

Tessa brushed back the blond strands that threatened to block her view as she shifted from side to side to look at the surrounding foliage. "I wish we could walk through these woods all the way back to our house."

"Yeah," Kris agreed. "This shade is a whole lot better than the hot sun. But we're gonna have to cross the open Prairie again to reach the other side."

The dirt road eventually turned north and presented the equestrians with a panoramic view of Paynes Prairie.

"Look at that!" Andi exclaimed. "I can see all the way across the Prairie from up here."

"See that tall building," Tessa pointed out. "I wonder if it's the university or maybe the Seagle Building downtown."

*Chapter 16*

"There's the apartments where we rescued Scout," Kris observed. "It's that first set of buildings just past the trees on the other side."

Andi gestured to a raised levee that stretched across the vast marshland. "There's the dike that Gina rode across. Let's follow it."

The girls urged their horses forward until they reached the steep slope where the land broke off sharply from the high hammock.

"Come on, let's run!" Andi yelled as she galloped down the escarpment and onto the earthen spine that elevated the girls and their horses above the surrounding marsh. The other two followed, and almost instantly, the three girls were blazing a new path across the soul of Paynes Prairie. They continued galloping for a long stretch until they felt their horses' feet sink into the wet earth, spewing clumps of mud with each rising hoof.

"Hold up!" Andi motioned. "It's gettin' too muddy to keep gallopin'."

"We made it almost halfway across," Tessa announced triumphantly as she signaled her pony to walk.

Kris nudged up her glasses as she strained to look at the dike ahead. "It still looks passable to me," she said.

"Yeah, it looks clear, but …," Tessa abandoned her thought when she realized that the mound she was looking at just a few feet from their path was not what it first appeared. "Oh, no, look at that," she pointed out. "It's an alligator, and it's buried itself in the mud." Tessa instinctively nudged her pony away from the reptile. "I sure hope Snuffy doesn't see it. He's scared of gators."

"There's another one," Andi called out as she pointed to the left.

Kris gasped. "Oh no, I think they're all around us."

A wave of worry spread across Tessa's face. "I can't let Snuffy see the gators, or he'll panic, and I could fall off like LeeAnne did. Can I get between you two, so your horses will block Snuffy if he tries to spook?"

"Sure," Andi agreed. "I'll lead, and you walk right behind me." Andi orchestrated this adventure, and she naturally assumed the leadership role.

"I'll follow right behind you," Kris offered to Tessa, "just like you did for me when we crossed the cattle gap."

Andi tried to shift her friends' attention from the threat of gators to a game of challenge. "Instead of gettin' nervous, let's just count all the gators we see."

Kris agreed. "We need to look for babies too," she added with a level of enthusiasm that Tessa didn't share. "They could be hidin' in the mud next to their mommas."

"If I'd known we'd be seein' all these gators, then I would've ridden Speedy," Tessa announced tensely. "He's not afraid of anything."

"Yeah, but you might not have gotten him to cross the cattle gap," Andi laughed.

*"And maybe I wouldn't be walking among gators in the middle of the Prairie,"* Tessa thought to herself.

Lucky for the girls, the intense heat caused the alligators to seek thermal refuge by laying in the shallow water and cool, wet earth. If the air had been cold and the water chilled, the reptiles would have been sunning on the same muddy spine that the cowgirls were now traversing.

Andi pointed to the right. "There's number 6 and 7 and 8."

"And 9 and 10 right back there," Kris added.

The levee was sinking lower, threatening to be engulfed by the bowels of the Prairie. The north end of the marsh was in

## Chapter 16

sight, but then again, the south end where they began their remote interior crossing was also visible, just further away from their targeted destination. Their game of discovering and tallying alligators started out fun, and briefly distracted the young explorers from the reality of their dangerous surroundings. But the newness of the game soon lost its appeal as the reality of their remoteness, and the uncertainty of their escape begin to sink in.

Tessa tried to summon more confidence. "I know there's lots of gators around us, but we can't turn around now. Otherwise, we'll be ridin' home in the dark."

Andi glanced back at her two friends. "We can make it," she reassured them. "We don't have too much further to go."

"Number 25." Kris called out from her stern position as she motioned left toward another alligator that the two in front had not seen.

Tessa halted abruptly and tensed as she shifted her gaze from one side of the wildness to the other. "Oh no, did you hear that?"

Andi looked around for the source of the noise. "It sounds like a boat motor."

"There ain't no one crazy enough but us to be out here in this swamp in the middle of the summer. And I sure don't see no boats out here." Kris wished she hadn't sounded quite so sarcastic.

Tessa pointed to the left. "I hear it again. It's coming from over there."

The girls looked left, but all they saw was a carpet of pickerelweed with its purple flowers reaching above its leaves.

"There it is again! Now it's coming from the right!" Kris called out in alarm.

The girls searched the other side, but again could only see an expansive mat of water-loving plants. "It sounds like an angry growl," Andi thought out loud.

And when the reptilian rumble sounded again, this time only 20 feet from where the cowgirls stood, Snuffy, who was in the middle position, began to shake his head and fidget back and forth.

"Oh no, I think Snuffy's about to spook," Tessa shuddered. "Keep walking," she demanded in a tone more alarming than they had ever heard from their toe-headed friend. "And keep us boxed in, so Snuffy doesn't take off," she added.

They continued their procession north, with the middle equestrian sandwiched in snuggly between the front and rear riders. Mud sucked at their horses' hooves as they journeyed along the vanishing dike. Another gator bellowed its dominance from a spot nearby.

"Wow, I just saw a gator yell!" Andi called out from her lead position. "It lifted its head, and when it opened its mouth and growled, water droplets bounced on top of its back!"

Unlike the leader ahead, Tessa wasn't impressed with the call of the gators. Rather, her tension level rose with each reptilian roar. "Keep going," she motioned nervously with the reins. "I just want out of here."

Andi tried to reassure her friend. "Those gators are out in the water, and as long as we stay up here, we won't have any problems. I can see the upper edge of the Prairie, and it's not too much further."

"Let's keep countin' gators," Kris suggested, hoping it would distract her nervous friend, and frankly, her equally nervous self. "Those bellowing gators were numbers 36, 37, and 38."

"Great," Tessa replied sarcastically.

*Chapter 16*

As the girls gazed out across the vast Prairie, they spotted gangly egrets whose white feathers contrasted sharply with the sea of green marsh plants. The long-legged wading birds were stealthily searching for frogs and fish and other aquatic morsels. Further ahead, a few dozen white ibis took wing in a clustered formation, abandoning their soggy surroundings where they had been foraging for worms. Most of the flock were adults with white feathers, but interspersed were brown and white mottled juveniles, and all with their diagnostic down-curved bills that are so efficient at plucking subterranean prey from the soggy earth.

Andi raised her arm and signaled for her two followers to stop. Up ahead a crane-like bird had just snagged a wiggling fish. The blue and gray heron secured its food in its deadly bill and swallowed it head first. The hunter then winged over to a more isolated part of the marsh away from the equine explorers. The girls remained motionless as they watched the large bird preen itself, lifting one lacy parasol and then another as it meticulously guided its bill along the collection of multi-colored feathers.

As they resumed their procession north, Tessa gasped when she spied a snake, decorated in all shades of mud, slide off the berm and disappear into the weeds, leaving no sign of its venomous presence. Tessa realized that a far larger tribe of reptiles surrounded her than she could truly comprehend.

A short time later Kris pointed to the right and called out, "there's number 52 and 53 over there."

The muddy trail was rapidly dissolving into the surrounding vastness of Paynes Prairie. "Water's startin' to cover the dike, but if we continue straight, we can stay on top of it," Andi reported. "Otherwise, we might step off into the deep water."

"Where the snakes and gators are," Tessa mumbled as she trailed close behind the leader.

"Number 75," Andi called out.

Kris, straddling a small mount, couldn't spot as many alligators as Andi could from her lead position on the tall Appaloosa. Kris was happy to walk single file, and she was content being last in line and trying to keep Tessa's nervous

*Chapter 16*

pony secured by the other two horses. Kris had started out brave, especially when they were galloping along the raised dike. She delighted in the adventure of riding somewhere new, and especially at crossing through the middle of Paynes Prairie where almost every other person in Gainesville would be scared to venture. But now she could barely distinguish between the shallow water that covered her path and the adjacent deeper water where the bellowing alligators resided. Although she would not voice it like Tessa had, she was nervous too. She worried about how deep the water would get before they reached the other side and whether they would find a way out. A short pony wading in water with alligators was enough to frighten even the bravest equestrian, and this Idylwild Cowgirl was no exception.

The girls continued along the narrow spine of what remained of their path to freedom. Then, to their collective relief, the dike's elevation slowly began to rise. Finally, they reached dry ground.

"I can't believe we made it across that gator-infested marsh," Tessa uttered. "I bet I'll have nightmares for weeks."

"One hundred and five," Andi reported as they ascended the steep slope. "That's how many gators we spotted."

Tessa was ready to leave all 105 gators behind and focus on a more pleasant topic. "Look at those huge oak trees," she said as she admired the woods around her. This is just as lovely as the uplands on the other side of the Prairie."

A crow cawed as it winged above the hammock, which set off a squirrel in a nearby tree. The furry rodent flicked its tail, barked its alarm, and bounded across the limbs.

Kris looked up at the shaking branches. "I think that squirrel just scolded us," she laughed.

Andi continued in her leadership position. "Let's follow this trail, and I bet it'll take us right to a gate."

The path widened and transitioned to a mowed woods road. The girls savored the shady, high dry ground, and the absence of so many reptiles. So what if the university's mascot is a gator. These cowgirls had just encountered nearly as many live alligators as the university's entire football team, the team called the *Florida Gators*.

After an enjoyable spell of following the woods road, Kris pointed up ahead. "Look! There's a gate."

The girls cued their mounts to trot, and when they reached the gate, Andi slid down from her horse and pulled on the clasp. "Oh no, it's locked."

"Check the hinges on the other end," Kris suggested. "Maybe we can lift the gate off its hinges."

"Don't look like it," Andi replied. "One hinge points up and the other points down. We can't slide the gate off with it that'a way."

"What are we gonna do?" Tessa asked.

Even Andi, the perpetual adventure-seeker, was ready for a rest. But for the sake of her less brave friends, she kept her face of encouragement. "Let's keep followin' the dirt road, and we'll probably find another gate, one that ain't locked."

The girls continued their journey north along the meandering and shaded dirt road. They didn't notice that several birds were singing – a tanager and a vireo and even a loud and boisterous hawk. But they did realize that the sun had dropped lower into the western sky and would soon be setting below the horizon.

"We have to find a way out of here real soon," Tessa warned. "It's gonna get dark and we'll be trapped in these woods."

*Chapter 16*

"We're only about a mile from home. I'm sure not willin' to cross that dike again," Kris asserted.

"Snuffy and I have seen enough gators today to last us for the rest of our lives," Tessa added. "I'd sleep in these woods before I'd walk back across that dike." But Tessa did not want to sleep in the woods. She yearned for her bedroom and her comfortable bed and the sweet smell of clean sheets that her mother sun-dried on the clothesline in the back yard. She silently wished she had declined the invitation to cross the dike through the middle of Paynes Prairie.

"Let's keep followin' the fence line," Andi suggested. "We're sure to come to another gate."

The girls urged their horses forward. Although the forest was just as picturesque as the woods they so admired in their neighborhood, the girls were fixated on escaping and had now lost sight of the natural beauty of the stately oaks, scattered magnolias, and even the tropical looking cabbage palms. They had only intended to accompany Jodi and her new horse, Scout, half way across Paynes Prairie so she could meet up with Claire. And then they would ride back to one of their houses for lunch. But their half day ride turned into a full days' journey, and the end was not yet in sight. The cowgirls were hungry, thirsty, tired, sunburned, and yearning to be home with their families.

They spotted a house up ahead and could see that its back yard extended down to the path where they were traveling. A fence separated the wilds of the forest from the tamer yard, and the house sat a full 200 feet from the fence.

"Is there a gate where we can go into the back yard?" Tessa asked.

Andi surveyed the surrounding parcel from the top of her long-legged mount. "Nope. I don't see one," she reported.

Kris slid down from her pony and handed the reins to Tessa. "Here, hold these while I see if anyone's home."

Tessa and Andi waited while Kris scaled the fence and jogged up to the house. The cowgirl knocked on the back door, pushed up her glasses as she fidgeted on the porch, and knocked again, this time more forcibly. She peeked through the window but saw only darkness. She pounded on the door again, but could not arouse a response. Hope turned to despair as she sulked back to her companions.

"We hafta keep lookin' for another way out," Andi instructed. "Let's keep goin'."

They rode another mile or so in search of an escape route. Daylight began to fade into dusk, and as if on cue, an army of mosquitoes launched their attack. The girls slapped and swatted, while the horses shook their heads, stomped their feet, and swished their tails in a futile attempt to escape the biting insects. The fear of alligators was now replaced with the annoyance of hundreds of stinging mosquitoes.

Andi called out excitedly as she pointed to the left. "Hey, look over there! A tree fell across the fence and knocked it down!"

Tessa wasn't encouraged. "There's tree branches covering the fence and woods on both sides. We can't get out there."

Kris's resourcefulness kicked in. "All we have to do is clear the branches away from the fence and make a path so we can jump over the tree and the fallen fence."

The trio began transforming the snarl of limbs and trees and sagging fence into an escape route. They snapped off branches from the fallen tree until they had created a path on both sides of the fence. Midway along the clearing was now a three-foot high cluster of branches, a tree trunk, and tangled barbed wire.

*Chapter 16*

"I'll go first," Andi offered as she untied the reins and swung onto her horse's back. She walked Bingo away from the downed fence, and when she was about 50 feet from the makeshift jump, she reined him around. She lifted her hands and kicked, and the gelding sprang into a canter. She aimed straight at the wall of debris, and Bingo, the largest and most athletic of the three mounts, sailed right over the fence jump.

Andi reined Bingo back to a walk and praised him for his bravery. She yelled back to the other two on the opposite side of the fence. "You have to kick your pony for all your worth and keep its head facing straight ahead! Else he might duck to the side. And don't look down at the jump," she instructed. "Look at me, and you can do it!"

Kris hollered back to Andi. "I'll try next. You made it look so easy!"

Like Andi, Kris found a starting point about 50 feet from the fence. She kicked her pony into a canter and clicked loudly. Patches labored into a bouncy trot and then a half-hearted lope. When she reached the obstacle, Patches stopped and cut sharply to the left.

Tessa was nervous wondering how her pony was going to jump over an obstacle that was nearly as tall as his short withers. And seeing her friends' horse refuse the jump frightened her more. Without a word, Tessa trotted away from the obstacle. When she was a full 200 feet away, she wheeled her mount around, and with the loudest and most deliberate cues she could muster, she commanded her Shetland into a gallop. As she raced toward the jump, she kicked and clicked and kept her eyes fixated straight ahead on the Appaloosa on the other side of the fence. Her determined and strong-willed pony hurtled over the three-foot fence. When they landed, she halted, jumped to the ground, and wrapped her arms around Snuffy's neck.

"Good job, Tessa!" Andi yelled. "Your little guy has the biggest heart I've ever seen!" She turned to Kris on the other side of the fence and barked her instructions. "You're gonna have to kick and yell at your horse like your life depends on it or you ain't gettin' out of here tonight. Understand? Patches' needs a lot more spirit to clear that fence."

Kris wasn't put off by her friend's bossiness. Rather, she appreciated Andi's instructions, especially if it would help land her on the opposite side of the fence. "I have an idea," Kris called back. "If we could follow you and Bingo over the jump then I bet Patches would go over it. She never wants to lead in a scary situation, but she's always willin' to follow."

"You mean you want me and Bingo to jump back over the fence again?" Andi asked in disbelief.

"Well yeah. I think that's the only way me and Patches are gettin' out of here."

"Oh, ok," Andi replied hesitantly. She maneuvered Bingo through the forest at a trot, and when she had a clear line to the jump, she cantered her mount straight toward the fence, where once again, Bingo sprang over the obstacle.

"Let's approach the fence just like Tessa did from way back there, so we have a long running start," Kris suggested.

The two girls trotted their horses away from the fence, and when they were a sufficient distance away, Andi again coached her friend. "Make sure you keep kickin' and clickin' the entire time. Keep her head pointed at the jump so she can't turn away. And when you're one stride away from the fence, reach up and grab mane so she can stretch her neck forward." She gazed at her long-time friend. "Are you ready?"

"Ready as I'll ever be!"

"OK. You gotta keep up with us."

*Chapter 16*

Andi pointed Bingo's head straight at the jump and kicked him into a powerful canter. Kris galloped in close pursuit of the leader, and as the athletes in front approached the jump, she watched the pair sail, for the third time, over the fence. Kris maintained her determination, and when her pinto began to hesitate, Kris slammed her heels into the pony's barrel. She reached half way up her horse's neck, grabbed a handful of mane, looked straight ahead at Tessa on the far side of the jump, and jammed her heels into her pony's sides one last time. And Patches leaped on the heels of Bingo, right over the three-foot jump.

"Yeah!" Tessa shouted. "You did it!"

As her pony transitioned to a walk, Kris wrapped her arms around Patches' neck and cried, "Thank you, thank you. You're the best pony ever!"

A cloak of darkness enveloped the girls as they emerged from the woods. "I'm ready to get home," Tessa mumbled. "That's a ride I don't ever want to repeat."

# Chapter 17

Jodi, Claire, and Mary Kate watched in amazement as the three girls – Andi, Kris, and Tessa - maneuvered their horses across the cattle gap and gained entrance onto the new State Park. Then the trio continued their trek southward to the Hill's farm, with Duke the dog tracking close behind.

"I hope they find the trail that takes 'em all the way across the Prairie," Mary Kate said as she gripped the reins of her rotund pony and dangled her legs freely from side to side.

Claire agreed. "Yeah, and I hope they find a way out once they reach the other side."

Jodi settled in on the far side of the mowed right-of-way while the two more seasoned riders positioned themselves between her and the highway. "Well they're the most determined, resourceful, and imaginative group of girls I've ever met," Jodi said as she glanced over at the other two riders. "They found me a $15 horse, helped build my fence, and gathered up horse supplies. And I'm just the new kid on the block. They'll find a way across, even if they have to dodge alligators and jump over fences." Little did the cowgirls know how true that last comment would be.

After they had ridden a mile or so south along the edge of the highway, Claire motioned to the left. "Here's our driveway."

The three girls reined their horses east and continued down a long narrow lane that bisected two expansive pastures.

*Chapter 17*

Jodi pointed at the field on the right. "Are those your cows?"

"Yep, those are my dad's," Claire nodded.

At that moment, a boisterous whinny echoed from the left pasture opposite the field that housed the cows. A sorrel horse with a crooked blaze and two white stockings pranced over to the fence next to the girls. His neck was arched, his ears pricked forward, and his nostrils flared as he strutted back and forth in an air of masculinity.

Scout jerked around to face the animated horse.

"That's Rainbow," Claire said. "He's Mr. Posey's horse."

"He's a stallion," Mary Kate announced.

Jodi watched as the ruler of his pasture paraded back and forth along the fence, high-stepping with each stride. His rounded neck bulged with powerful muscles, the strength amplified as his coat's scarlet sheen reflected in the sun. His rounded jowls also spoke of strength, and his animation and loud whinnies demanded his audience's full attention.

"He's beautiful," Jodi said as she admired the magnificent animal in all his glory.

"Oh, he's just showing off," Mary Kate said. "He's not usually like that."

Jodi was riveted on his beauty, yet intimidated by the powerhouse of strength that flaunted back and forth in the pasture beside her. "Have you ever ridden him?" she asked somewhat sheepishly.

Claire nodded. "I used to ride him all the time before I got Shotsie, but he's spirited and barn-sour, and he shakes his head up and down. He's not nearly as fun to ride as Shotsie boy is."

"Do you keep your horses in the same pasture with Rainbow?" Jodi asked.

Mary Kate shook her head. "Oh no, he would fight 'em. But he's fine with the cows out there," she said as she gestured to a small herd that was grazing in the same field with Rainbow.

"Let's give the horses some water and then ride in the pasture with the cows," Claire suggested. "That'll be horse training exercise number 1."

Jodi was alarmed. "Ride with the cows and Rainbow-the-stallion?"

"No," Claire replied. "We'll ride in the other pasture with just the cows." She continued with a partial description of her horse-training techniques. "I like to ride Shotsie around things on the farm that might be spooky, so he gets used to them and then he's less bothered by new sights out on the trail. Since he's used to walking through a herd of cows, then hopefully he won't spook when we encounter a deer or other wild animals."

Jodi nodded. "Oh, I see." She hesitated a moment as she recalled an event worth sharing. "Tessa told me she once rode Speedy right into the kitchen where her mom was cookin' and asked for a carrot."

Mary Kate gazed at Jodi in disbelief. "Really?"

"Yep." Jodi nodded. "Her mom yelled at her to get the horse out of the house before he left a big mess on the floor. And she didn't mean dirt."

"I could see Tessa ridin' her little pony into the kitchen," Claire laughed, "but big ole Speedy?"

"Yeah, Speedy'll do just about anything she asks him to. He's a retired show horse you know, so he doesn't get excited about new sights," Jodi explained.

Claire chuckled. "Well, I ain't never heard of no one ridin' their horse into the house. Just leave it to Tessa."

*Chapter 17*

When they reached the water trough, they took turns letting their horses drink. "I'm gonna hose King off and turn him loose in the pasture," Mary Kate said. "I'll see ya inside."

Claire and Jodi rode their horses in the pasture opposite the field that housed the stallion, through the knee-high Bahia toward the cows. The fifteen or so bovines paused briefly from grazing to watch the approaching riders before they buried their heads back in the tall grass. Scout froze at the sight of the cows and stood at full alert.

"Let her look at the cows and pet her neck to comfort her," Claire instructed.

"This is our first cow encounter," Jodi said nervously. "I hope she doesn't take off running."

"If she does, just hang on and try to stop her. But she looks like she's startin' to relax. Let's make a wide circle around the cows," Claire suggested.

The two looped around the herd, keeping a large separation between the apprehensive horse and the tranquil cows. Scout slowly settled and began to focus her attention on the other new surroundings. When they had completely encircled the herd, Claire coached her visitor. "Now let's make another loop around the cows, and this time we'll walk the horses a bit closer."

"Good plan," Jodi agreed.

"If we do this every day while you're here, then by the third day, Scout may ignore the cows, just like Shotsie does."

Jodi smiled as she reached down and stroked her mount's dun-colored neck. "I want her to be calm and not spooky. I was pretty scared this morning when the birds flew up and she took off running. Luckily, Andi and Bingo stopped her before she ran into the road."

"In a few weeks, she'll be a different horse, and you'll be more a comfortable rider," Claire reassured her. "Come on, let's head to the barn so we can hose the horses and turn them out to graze and rest."

As they approached the house, Claire's mother came out to greet them. "Hi, Momma," Claire said as she waved. "This is Jodi."

"Hi, girls. Pleased to meet you, Jodi" she said as she smiled at the visitor. "Did y'all have a nice ride?"

"Yes mam," they both answered.

Claire began explaining the other girls' riding arrangement. "Andi, Kris, and Tessa rode with Jodi across the Prairie so she wouldn't have to ride alone for her first Prairie crossing. Then they cut across the cattle gap through the new trail entrance and said they were gonna ride back along a raised dike that crosses through the middle of the Prairie."

Seriousness spread across Jodi's face as she listened to the story. "I sure hope they make it all the way across."

"Yeah, and I hope they find a way out once they get to the other side," Claire added.

Claire's mom shared the girls' concerns. "You should call Tessa tonight to make sure she and the others made it home safely."

After dinner, Claire telephoned Tessa to hear about their return ride across the Prairie. But to her alarm, Tessa was not home yet. The other two girls had not returned either, Mrs. Brown told her. Mr. Brown was out looking for the missing riders. Claire described the route the three girls had taken and when Mrs. Brown asked where the girls could be, Claire had to admit she had no idea.

*Chapter 17*

Claire looked frightened as she hung up the phone. "Tessa and the others haven't made it home yet. There's no telling where they are."

"They could be stuck in the middle of the Prairie," Jodi replied, equally unnerved by the news.

"Or they could be ridin' along the highway in the dark." Claire called out to her dad. "Can you please drive us across the Prairie so we can look for them?"

"Sure can," he replied.

Mr. Hill eased the truck off the highway next to the fence where the three cowgirls had gained entrance into the State Park earlier in the day. "I don't expect they'd still be here, but it doesn't hurt to call out for 'em," he said.

Jodi and Claire yelled into the darkness for their missing friends. But there was no response, not until an owl hooted its lonesome call from somewhere in the distant blackness.

"Let's drive across the Prairie and look for 'em," Mr. Hill suggested.

Jodi braced her shoulders against the seat of the truck and shivered. "Oh, I would be so scared to ride across the Prairie at night. Just think how many snakes there are out there."

"And gators too," Claire added.

They saw no sign of the missing riders along the edge of the highway that crossed the expansive Paynes Prairie. Once they were across the Prairie, Mr. Hill turned off the highway and onto Crown Road. Through the glare of the headlights, they spotted the three equestrians up ahead.

"Hey, we were worried about you," Claire shouted as she rolled down the truck window. "What took you so long to get back?"

"I'll tell you all about it tomorrow," Tessa said wearily. "Right now, we just want to get home and away from all these pesky mosquitoes."

Claire waved. "OK, we're glad you're safe. I'll call you tomorrow."

As they drove off, Jodi said, "I wonder if they're telling ghost stories."

"I'm willin' to bet they had more than their share of frightening experiences for one day," Mr. Hill replied. "They probably don't need any more scary stories tonight."

## Chapter 18

The next morning after breakfast Jodi, Claire, and Mary Kate hurried to the barn to feed, groom, and tack up their horses. The girls were delighted to see Scout grazing near the two resident horses in the middle of the pasture.

"Come on," Claire motioned. "Let's catch the horses."

"Here's a carrot for each of them," Mary Kate offered, as she handed a horse treat to the other two girls.

They groomed their mounts meticulously, picked their hooves, and brushed through their mane and tail until every tangle had been disassembled. Scout's condition was improving with every week that Jodi doted on her. And apparent to Claire and the other cowgirls' trained eyes, Scout was transforming from an ignored, and soon-to-be castaway to a loved and fussed-over member of Jodi's immediate family.

"Wanna ride to George's pond and take the horses swimmin'?" Claire asked the other two girls.

"Sure," Mary Kate agreed. "Let's stop at Mr. Beckwith's Gun Store for a drink on our way over there," she suggested.

"Can we ride around the cows first so Scout can get used to them again?" Jodi asked. Jodi was learning from Claire, the amateur horse teacher, that repetition was an important aspect of horse training.

"Sure," Claire nodded.

Flanked on both sides by the other two horses, Scout was fully alert to the grazers as she circled around the herd in the adjacent pasture.

"Just don't yell 'boo' or she might take off," Jodi said anxiously.

The heifers and their nearby calves ignored the horses and continued chewing the sweet grass, oblivious to their inclusion in the horse-training exercise. After two more loops around the herd, Scout finally settled and eyed the cows as almost commonplace. The green horse now directed her attention to the farm's other newness – the tractor implements parked in the pasture, the pole barn that was stacked with hay bales, and even an elderberry bush that sagged from the weight of its prolific production of flowers.

"She's gonna settle down soon," Claire reassured her friend. "You'll see."

Mary Kate turned to Jodi. "Have you ever ridden Scout through a creek?"

Jodi shook her head. "Not yet, but I'm ready to try."

A narrow flow-way bisected the Hill farm, transporting water from its southern reaches northward until it emptied its cache onto Paynes Prairie. When rain events were plentiful, the creek swelled, and the water flowed with a purpose, in a hurry to reach its marshy destination. But during dry periods, the stream retreated, like it was holding its breath and preventing what little water it had from escaping its banks. Since evaporation was in full summer force, the watercourse was shallow and with an almost imperceptible flow. The riders approached the creek at its most inviting spot where water plants were absent and the bottom clearly visible.

"This is where the cows cross the creek," Claire pointed out.

*Chapter 18*

Scout paused when she reached the stream. She arched her neck, pricked her ears forward, and gazed down at the shallows with a sign of uncertainty so characteristic of a green horse. Jodi let her horse examine the new terrain and then nudged the mare to follow the others through the water. Scout tiptoed cautiously at first and then extended her stride as she hurried through her first known water crossing.

Claire's praise was intended for both horse and rider. "That was great, Jodi. Well done. Pet her and let her know she did good, and let's cross it again." They traversed the creek three more times, with the final crossing led by Jodi and Scout.

Jodi beamed from her accomplishments so far that morning - riding around the herd of cows and walking through a creek. Those were the baby steps of horse training, but critical to eventually producing a seasoned, bomb-proof, trail horse. Jodi wanted a trustworthy mount, not one that bolted when birds flew out of a bush, and she was learning how to teach her horse to become a dependable equine partner.

Mary Kate recognized Jodi's accomplishments too. "Scout did great with the water. Now the next water adventure will be swimming with a gator."

"A gator!" Jodi exclaimed, "I don't know about that."

"Oh, it's just a small one," Claire laughed. "You probably won't even notice it."

Jodi tried to sound brave. "If you're not worried then I'll try not to be either."

With Duke following at their horses' heels, the three girls journeyed south to George's Pond, staying within the grassy mowed right-of-way of Highway 441. After a mile or so, Mary Kate pointed to the opposite side of the road. "There's Beckwith's Gun Store. Let's cross the road and buy a soft drink."

They halted their horses, and as they waited for a break in the traffic, Claire turned toward the dog that had been following close behind. "Duke, Duke sit," she ordered. When the setter realized he was being signaled to, he perked up his ears and complied with his owner's command. After a few more cars passed by, Claire motioned to the other two riders. "The road's clear in both directions. Let's cross. Duke, come," she added as she beckoned to the setter.

After they crossed the four-lane divided highway, Mary Kate pointed to the far side of a small concrete building. "There's a shady spot where we can sit and drink our sodas." She turned to her sister. "If you'll hold King's reins, I'll buy our drinks."

"Sure." Claire reached into her pocket and pulled out four quarters. "Here's enough money for all three drinks. I'll have a sprite. Jodi, what do you want?"

"Root beer if they have it."

Mary Kate returned from the store holding three canned drinks. An older man followed her out and smiled as he greeted the cowgirls.

"Good morning young ladies. And how are y'all today?"

"Fine, thank you," Claire nodded. "Mr. Beckwith, this is our friend, Jodi. She lives on the other side of the Prairie, and she's visiting for a few days."

The proprietor of Beckwith's Gun Store, Harry Beckwith, was a muscular man in his mid-forties. He wore a close-cut buzz haircut, a carefully trimmed mustache, and wire-rimmed glasses. "Well howdy, Miss Jodi. I'm mighty pleased to meet you." Turning to Claire, he chuckled, "I see you remembered your money this time."

"Yes sir, thanks to my sister for reminding me."

*Chapter 18*

"Are you all sneaking through the YMCA property to George's Pond again?"

"Yes," Claire replied sheepishly. "We want to swim the horses, and Jodi's never taken her horse swimmin' before."

"You girls be careful and watch out for gators," he said as he winked at Mary Kate, the youngest in the group.

After Mr. Beckwith had returned to his store, Mary Kate held up her soda and sloshed the remaining contents around in the can. Her rotund pony perked up his ears and stretched his nose over to the can. "I saved some coke for you," she cooed. Mary Kate held her drink up to her horse's mouth, and as soon as King felt the coolness of the can against his muzzle, he began mouthing his lips. Mary Kate poured the remaining drink into his whiskered-covered, outstretched lips. The Welch pony slurped some of the soda but slobbered most of the brown liquid down her raised arm.

Jodi laughed as she handed her drink with its remaining contents to Mary Kate. "Does he like root beer?"

"Yep, he'll drink just about anything. He once drank Uncle Ken's beer," she laughed.

"And after that first sip of beer, he followed Uncle Ken around the front yard tryin' to get more," Claire chuckled.

After the girls and King-the-pony had finished their drinks, they continued their journey to George's Pond. A short time later, they reached a leaning white sign, lettered YMCA, which signified the entrance to the summer camp and the route to their covert swimming hole. The riders followed the tree line that led downslope to the pond. A clearing along the shore signified the camp's narrow beach and the only access to the water.

Claire motioned to a grassy spot about 50 feet upslope from the water that was shaded by nearby sweetgums. "We can leave our tack there while we swim." Remounting their horses bareback, the cowgirls urged their horses toward the sandy beach at the edge of George's Pond.

"Take it slow and easy," Claire instructed Jodi, "so Scout can get used to the water. She'll probably want to stop and drink."

"But if she starts pawing," Mary Kate cautioned, "then kick her to go. That means she's about to lie down and roll."

Jodi shot Mary Kate a look of disbelief as if to question the remote possibility that a horse would even try to roll in the water.

Claire confirmed her sister's comment. "Yep, she really could roll," Claire laughed. "Just be ready to kick her if she starts to buckle at the knees."

Without hesitation, Shotsie and King obeyed their riders' nudges and waded into the warm, tea-colored water. When the water depth was knee high, which was much sooner for close-to-the-ground King, the Welch pony, than for long-legged Shotsie, the horses halted, stretched out their necks, and slurped the tannic liquid. Duke followed the girls out for a short distance, drank from the pond, and plopped down in the water. Straddling Scout's back, Jodi remained on the sandy bank while she gazed at the tranquil pond. This time, instead of the rider cueing the horse, Scout sent her own signal to Jodi. The dun stretched out her neck, tugged the leather reins, and walked toward the water. She paused for a moment at the water's edge and then ventured out until she was poised next to King. Then she began splashing the water with her nose.

Jodi tensed. "What's she doing? Is she about to roll?"

"No," Claire laughed. "She's just playin' in the water."

After the horses were fully hydrated, the equestrians urged their mounts toward the deeper reaches of the pond, and when the water depth reached the horses' belly, the horses began their

## Chapter 18

equine version of dog paddling. The girls gripped their mounts' mane and let the horses gently propel them through the water.

"Isn't this fun?" Mary Kate exclaimed.

"Yes! This is great." Jodi laughed.

Mary Kate called out to her older sister. "Hey, Claire! Will you hold King's reins for me?"

"Sure thing," Claire replied.

Mary Kate tossed the leathers to her sister and then slowly stood up on King's round back. She stretched her arms above her head and dove into the water. King stood motionless as Mary Kate's pint-size body produced a meager splash.

Claire handed the leathers back to her sister. "I think it's time to leave now. Looks like the gator's finally shown up," she announced as she gestured to where a small pair of dark bulges protruded just above the water surface about a hundred feet from where the girls were swimming.

Jodi strained to locate the gator. "Gosh, it's small. I wouldn't have even noticed it if you hadn't pointed it out."

The girls directed the horses over to the pile of tack that they had left in the grass. "Let's sit here awhile so the horses can graze before we head back," Claire suggested.

The trio relaxed in the grassy field that overlooked the pond, still cooled by their wet clothes and refreshing swim. Jodi silently marveled at the soothing sounds the horses made as they mouthed the sweet foliage. She savored her new life with her new horse. This was more magnificent than she ever had imagined.

Claire broke the silence. "Hey Jodi, did you know today is the summer solstice?"

Jodi shook her head. "No."

"What's that?" Mary Kate, the youngest cowgirls asked.

"It's the longest day of the year," her sister replied.

Mary Kate looked confused. "Really? How long is it today?"

Claire shifted to her most authoritative and serious face. "Twenty-five hours long," she announced. "All other days are twenty-four hours long, but on the summer solstice, it's twenty-five hours long."

## Chapter 18

Mary Kate wrinkled her brow and squinted. "Really? How's that?"

Claire could not maintain her composure, and when she tried to stifle her giggles, Jodi burst out laughing.

"Your sister's teasing you. All days are twenty-four hours long. There are just more daylight hours today, which makes it the longest day of the year," Jodi explained.

"And more hours for us to explore with our horses," Claire added.

After a relaxing rest in the shade of the sweetgums, the girls tacked up their horses and departed the tranquil setting of George's Pond and the resident alligator that had disappeared under the tannic water. Duke, their faithful companion, followed close behind.

The cowgirls were heading home along the eastern edge of the highway's grassy right-of-way when they reached a series of houses whose front yards bordered the road. Two dogs charged out from between the houses and ran straight at the riders. When the attackers realized there was a more vulnerable target, they altered their course and charged the setter. Duke bolted sideways and ran away from the attacking dogs straight into the highway.

"Duke, come!" Claire yelled. Her shout was met with the piercing sound of a car horn and squealing brakes. They watched in horror as a man in a small convertible jerked from one lane to the other to try and avoid hitting Duke. But the right front corner of the car struck the dog. Duke yelped loudly and was thrown to the edge of the pavement.

"Oh, Duke!" Claire cried as she kicked her horse toward the injured dog. She leaped down, and still holding the reins, reached out to comfort her companion. As she started to stroke his head, Duke groaned and stumbled backward. "It's ok

Duke," Claire said, as warm tears began flowing down her cheeks. "You'll be ok."

The driver in the black Sportster steered his car to the side of the highway and ran back to check on the injured dog. The man looked stricken. "I'm so sorry. I tried to avoid hitting him, but he just darted right out in front of me!"

Claire briefly locked eyes with the man as she tried to control her emotions. "It wasn't your fault Mister. He was running from those mean dogs."

"Can I take him home for you?" the man asked. "Where do you live?"

Claire pointed straight ahead. "My driveway's the first one after the big curve up ahead. Look for a black mailbox on the right that says '*Hill*' on it." As the man gently lifted the injured dog and placed him in the front seat of his car, Claire called out, "Careful, please be careful with him." And pausing to wipe the tears from her face, she added, "Thank you, Mister, for takin' Duke home for me. We'll get there as quickly as we can."

The three girls trotted their horses along the far edge of the highway until they reached the black mailbox that signified the farm's entrance. As they approached the house, they saw the man standing in the front yard talking to Mrs. Hill. And then, most unexpectedly, Duke began barking and wagging his tail and bolted out to greet the approaching riders.

"Oh Duke, I'm so glad you're ok!" Claire cried as she slid off her horse and hugged her dog. Tears once again clouded her eyes, but this time they were tears of joy as she realized her faithful canine companion would survive this harrowing experience.

## Chapter 19

The girls were more subdued on the final day of Jodi's visit, and instead of rushing out after breakfast to ride the horses, they remained indoors with Duke. And the dog relished the extra attention he received.

It was early afternoon when the girls finally decided to leave the house. "Let's just ride around the farm and keep it easy," Claire suggested as they strolled out to the pasture to retrieve their mounts. "I want to stay away from the highway today."

"Yeah," Jodi agreed. "Scout and I could use an easier day, especially since we have a long ride home tomorrow."

With Mary Kate joining them, the three girls reined their horses through the small herd of cows so Scout could once again acclimate to the sights and sounds of livestock. Then they rode through the creek, first at a walk and then a trot.

"Now let's canter through the water," Claire suggested. The girls cued their horses into a lope and aimed for the water crossing. Claire yelled back to Jodi, "Keep your legs on her and aim right at the creek!" All three horses plunged through the shallow water sending spray in every direction.

"Let's ride the trail around the back woods and then be done with our ride for today," Claire suggested.

"Yeah, that will be enough riding for me," Jodi agreed.

The girls set off east along the dirt road that squeezed between two pastures. A small bird was hunting for grasshoppers from his perch on the fence. He flashed his azure back as he winged up to a higher stakeout position. "Hey, there's a bluebird," Claire pointed out as the insect eater realigned himself on a nearby tree branch. After becoming fascinated with the bird rookery, Claire challenged herself to learn the birds around the farm. She could now recognize that particular species as an Eastern Bluebird. However, she was still too elementary in her knowledge to know that this brightly clad male was feathered in his most eye-popping plumage, the attire he acquired during the breeding season so he could win over a female.

When they reached the woods at the far eastern end of the farm, the trio turned north and followed the narrow grassy lane that encircled the flatwoods. The sunlight became subdued as they transitioned from the open pasture to the shaded piney woods. Pine trees – both loblolly and slash – punctuated the forest and were interrupted by an occasional loblolly bay, laurel oak, or red maple. Saw palmettos and various acid-loving shrubs formed a dense lower stratum that prevented any smaller plants from emerging from the forest floor.

As they traversed the far side of the pine forest, the most remote section of the farm, a movement on the trail up ahead caught Claire's attention. She motioned for the others to halt and then signaled them to silence.

"It's a fox," Claire whispered. "It's huntin' for food. Either it doesn't know we're here or it isn't scared of the horses."

As the girls quietly watched the hunter, Mary Kate asked, "I wonder what it's lookin' for?"

Claire whispered her reply. "Maybe rabbits or snakes or mice."

"Or even birds," Jodi practically mouthed so she wouldn't frighten the fox.

## Chapter 19

"How can a fox catch a bird when it could just fly off?" Mary Kate quietly asked.

Claire explained. "A fox could catch a baby turkey as it's walking on the ground, or other birds that are still in the nest and haven't learned to fly."

The girls watched as the stealth hunter sniffed the base of a dogfennel clump and then advance to a coppice of myrtles, where again it probed the bushes with its scent-sensitive nose. From their elevated position, the equestrians watched the fox search from one potential prey hiding spot to another. When the canine emerged into a sunny spot, they saw silver specks reflect off its soot-colored back. A furry ring of rust, like a bushy scarf, encircled its neck. The hunter was slight, barely larger than Jodi's house cat, and its long bushy tail further accentuated its scant body.

Without warning, the petite but fierce predator leaped up in the air and then sprang onto a target that was invisible to the observers. It pounced again, jerking first its right paw at the ground, then it's left, and then lunging into the brambles. After several long seconds, the hunter retracted its head and turned sideways where the girls could see a small mammalian body with a pencil-thin tail hanging from its muzzle.

"It caught a mouse," Mary Kate whispered to the others. The canine suddenly disappeared behind a myrtle bush with a death grip on its next meal.

"Let's turn around and walk back," Claire suggested. "Then we won't disturb the fox while it eats its food."

The others agreed.

Jodi planned to ride Scout home the next day. After three continuous days of riding with Claire and Mary Kate, she felt more confident on her new horse. But she was still not comfortable riding alone next to the highway all the way across Paynes Prairie back to her house. "I'm glad you're gonna ride with me and that Tessa's gonna meet us too," Jodi said to Claire.

"I'm staying at Tessa's house tomorrow night," Claire explained to Jodi, "and we're riding to Terwilliger Pond the next day. So I'll ride with you all the way across the Prairie tomorrow."

Mary Kate jokingly cautioned the two girls. "Don't try a new route across Paynes Prairie. Or you might not make it."

"Don't worry," Jodi laughed. "We're stickin' to the side of the road. No middle-of-the-Prairie explorin' for me."

The cowgirls couldn't predict the threats that awaited Claire and Tessa at Terwilliger Pond, dangers comparable to forging through the middle of the gator-infested Paynes Prairie.

## Chapter 20

The next morning, Claire and Jodi journeyed north along the grassy right-of-way of Highway 441 across Paynes Prairie. Mary Kate and Duke-the-dog remained behind.

As they approach the bird rookery, Claire observed, "The young egrets and herons sure are growing fast."

Jodi nodded as she admired the island of colorful animation created by the nesting birds.

"Let's trot for a while," Claire suggested. "Just a slow, relaxed jog."

"Sure," Jodi concurred.

"Keep Scout's head bent slightly to the right, away from the highway, just in case she spooks."

Jodi nodded as she nudged her mount into a trot. "She feels more relaxed than when I rode her to your house just a few days ago."

"Good." Claire smiled as she moved in rhythm with her horse's two-beat stride. "You've put a lot of miles on her in the last few days. She's more settled and you're a more confident rider."

The girls trotted a long stretch until they met up with their friends – Tessa, Andi, and Kris. After a brief chat, the five equestrians all headed north together.

"Did you see any animals on your ride over?" Claire asked the others.

"No, thank goodness," Tessa replied. "I've seen enough gators to last me a lifetime."

"The only animals we saw," said Jodi, "were the birds in the rookery."

"I hear you're training your horses to be hunter jumpers," Claire joked.

Tessa turned to Andi. "Bingo's the best jumper ever. He's the one that got us out of the woods."

"Yeah," Kris laughed. "But Andi had something to do with our rescue too."

"That's a good thing," Tessa said, "because it was Andi who got us into that mess in the first place."

Andi lifted her shoulders. "I think I'll take Bingo to a jumping show. You'd like that, wouldn't you, ole boy?" She laughed as she reached down and stroked his muscular neck. "You could race around the ring and leap over all the jumps on the course."

Tessa couldn't resist ribbing Kris. "Maybe they have a pairs class and you and Patches could follow Bingo around the jump course."

"That'd be the only way I could get this pony over any jumps," Kris laughed. "She's a sweetheart but she sure ain't no athlete like Bingo is."

Claire added to the teasing. "Hey, Kris, at least she's not five-gaited."

Kris shot Claire a puzzled look. "What do you mean, five-gaited?"

"Walk, trot, stumble, stagger, and fall!" Claire replied.

*Chapter 20*

The friends all laughed at the joke. Kris didn't mind them poking fun at her little pinto. She loved Patches, even with her ornery shortcomings.

They crossed the north boundary of Paynes Prairie, ascended the slope toward Gainesville, and continued past several driveways.

Andi turned to admire the recently rescued horse. "She's turnin' into a mighty fine ridin' horse."

"Look!" Jodi exclaimed as she pointed to the right. "That's where we rescued Scout. If it wasn't for Kris suggesting I buy her from the man, I might still be without a horse." Jodi could not have been happier.

The girls continued north past their normal turn off to the Idylwild neighborhood. They cut through a wide grassy field, crossed Williston Road, and continued their journey along a dirt road that led them to the restaurant's side entrance.

As the girls entered the parking lot of Sonny's Bar-B-Q Restaurant, they saw a plume of blue-gray smoke rising from the massive brick chimney. The tantalizing aroma of Bar-B-Q permeated the air. They reined their horses past the parked cars to the service area behind the building.

"It sure is nice that they built a hitching post for us back here," Kris said as she led her pony over to the posts that the restaurant manager had installed specifically for the cowgirls. "Just wish it was big enough for all five horses."

"Three of us can tie to the hitching post, and the other two can tie to the wooden fence," Andi suggested.

The girls were ushered to a table by a rotund, motherly-looking server who walked way too slow for the hungry girls. She motioned them to the fifth table back, right next to a window. They were grateful for the hitching post and appreciated sitting next to a window where they could view almost the entire parking lot, but they would have preferred to see the horses that were tied up in the back of the restaurant behind the kitchen.

The girls wanted to eat more than their limited money would allow, so each placed her minimal order – French fries and water, or garlic bread and a coke, or a barbecue sandwich. When the server delivered their order, she handed Andi, the tallest and oldest looking cowgirl, a handful of carrots. "These are for your horses," she smiled.

"Thank you very much," Andi replied.

After the delicious but not quite filling meal, the girls paid for their food and strolled out back to retrieve their horses.

Andi was the first to see the hitching post. "Oh, no, Bingo's gone!"

The other horses stood tied by their bridles, but absent was the tallest and most athletic horse of the herd. Only his bridle remained.

"Bingo's done pulled off his bridle and left you!" Kris exclaimed.

"Quick, let's go find him!" Tessa hollered.

The girls fed their horses the carrots and swung up on their mounts. Andi grabbed the dangling bridle that should have been attached to her horse's spotted face and jumped up on Speedy behind Tessa. The girls instantly formed a search posse as they backtracked along the dirt road.

Andi was nervous, and when she was nervous or excited, she fidgeted. She just couldn't keep her body from rocking or her legs from wiggling back and forth. Her natural reaction, had she been aboard her own horse, would be to squeeze her legs, just a smidgen because that's all it took to communicate to Bingo. And her responsive horse would have jumped to attention, ready to comply with his high-strung rider's signal to

## Chapter 20

accelerate. Often though, Bingo could just sense Andi's nervous energy, and without any cue from his rider, he would telepathically spring into a faster gate. This was part of the unspoken language between horse and rider.

Andi could not control her nervousness as she rode tandem behind Tessa in search of her missing horse. She willed her body to hold still, but that internal bouncing wouldn't stop. She tried to restrain her legs, but they instinctively kept gripping and squeezing Speedy's barrel in a manner that shouted, *Go Faster!* The palomino was unfazed by his passenger's jingling legs, and he continued to plod along. Finally, Andi couldn't contain herself.

"Is this as fast as your horse goes?" she almost shouted even though Tessa's ear was only a few inches in front of her.

"Come on Speedy, live up to your name for once," Tessa laughed good-naturedly as she kicked his cream-colored sides. "We gotta missin' horse to find."

The lazy mount notched up his stride just enough to satisfy his rider and her passenger, but no more, and without any enthusiasm. This retired show horse had been around the block too many times. It took more than a missing horse to rev up this retiree.

The posse had traveled a quarter of a mile along the dirt road, half its distance to the intersection with Williston Road when Kris spotted the first signs. "Look, I bet those horse prints are Bingo's."

"Yep," Andi agreed. "They look like Bingo's alright. I bet he's headed home."

Without turning around, Tessa laughed at her passenger. "He doesn't want a repeat of his ride across the Prairie dike, so he decided to take matters into his own hands, or hooves."

"I don't blame him," Kris concurred. "I don't want to repeat that experience either. Once was more than enough for me."

They followed the single line of prints along the dirt road to the stop sign at Williston Road. "Looks like he crossed right here," Jodi pointed out. "I sure hope he looked both ways."

"We can't follow his tracks anymore since there's a grassy field on the other side. Let's ride to my house and hope he's waitin' for us there," Andi suggested.

The posse pursued the path that they hoped the fugitive had taken. And when they arrived at Andi's house a long 15 minutes later, there stood Bingo, still outfitted in a bareback pad but minus his corresponding bridle.

"Boy am I glad to see you!" Andi shouted as she slid off Tessa's palomino and skipped over to her horse.

Kris laughed. "You've pulled so many pranks on your horse and on us too. It was his turn to get back at you."

"Well, what're we waiting for?" Andi beckoned, as she placed the bridle onto Bingo's face. "Let's go ridin'!"

The pack drifted out to Crown Road, their favorite thoroughfare, with no destination in mind. As they strolled along, Gina pedaled up from behind on her bicycle. "Hey there!" she shouted.

Kris looked back at Gina. "Where are you headin'?"

"I'm going to Mr. Taylor's pasture to ride Buck." Gina pedaled her bike faster, weaved past the group of horses, and pulled up to the lead position. "Wanna follow me over to the pasture so we can ride together?"

Andi squeezed Bingo into a trot and overtook Gina. "Sure, we'll ride with you, but you'll have to catch me if you want to lead."

Gina pedaled harder, but she was no match for Andi and her spirited Appaloosa. Andi slowed Bingo to a walk and held out

## Chapter 20

her left arm. "Catch up with me and grab my arm and I'll pull you faster." Gina stretched her right arm up and locked hands with Andi. "Hold on!" Andi shouted.

Andi signaled Bingo to trot, and her obedient mount transitioned from his brisk walk to an animated jog. With their hands clasped together, Gina pedaled her bike faster to stay synchronized with the rapidly spinning bike pedals.

"Hold on Gina, we're goin' faster!" Andi yelled. She gripped Gina's hand tighter so Gina couldn't let go, and kicked Bingo into a canter.

"I can't keep up with the pedals!" Gina shouted. She lifted her bare feet and held them straight out while the bike pedals hurled violently around in circles.

The others watched from behind as the bicyclist and equestrian, joined by their hands, rocketed down the dirt road. When the pair was traveling at top speed, Andi slowed Bingo a notch, and without signaling to Gina, slung her arm and released her grip on Gina's hand. Gina was slung forward, bicycle pedals spinning even faster, as she careened ahead on the narrow dirt road.

"Whoa!" Gina shouted as she tried to maintain control of her wobbling bicycle. "Whoa!" When Gina finally regained command of her bike, she looked back at Andi. "Why did you do that? You could've killed me!"

"I knew you could hang on," Andi laughed.

When they reached Mr. Taylor's pasture, Gina leaned her bike against the fence and set off to retrieve her horse from the back of the overgrown pasture. The other girls led their horses to the water trough.

"I sure am glad I don't keep Scout in this pasture anymore," Jodi said. "I just love having her in my own back yard."

"Hey, let's play hide-and-go-seek," Kris suggested. "This pasture's plenty big enough, and there's lots of places to hide with all the weeds and bushes."

"Good idea," Tessa agreed. "Where should the home base be?"

"Somewhere in the center of the pasture," Andi said. She pointed to a cluster of cabbage palms and small trees. "How about those trees over there?" The others agreed.

Tessa gathered six small twigs, all about the same length, except one that was notably shorter than the others. She held them so they all projected up from her clasped hand. "Everyone draw a stick," she instructed, "and whoever gets the shortest one has to stand at home base with your eyes shut and count to 100. Everyone else finds a place to hide with their horse."

Jodi drew the shortest stick. She navigated Scout over to the collection of palms and shrubs that defined home base, closed her eyes, and began counting. The other riders dispersed to find hiding spots that would conceal both them and their much larger horse.

This was not a new game for Jodi. She had played hide-and-go-seek with her brother and cousins, and even at a friend's birthday party last year, but she had never played it on horseback. When Jodi finished counting, she shouted, "Ready or not, here I come!" She circled around home base staying close and hoping to tag anyone who tried to dash back to the safe zone. But when she ventured over to the north side, the side closest to Rocky Point Road, Andi shot out from her hiding spot and galloped to the designated safe location. Jodi had no chance at catching the sprinting horse and rider. Jodi rode further out into the pasture looking for the other concealed targets. All at once, three riders dashed out from their hiding spots and rushed toward home base. Gina and her horse, Buck were fast and

## Chapter 20

easily outran Jodi without being tagged. Tessa and Claire were on slower horses and a more even match. Jodi focused on Tessa and her sluggish mount, and angled back toward home base, tagging Tessa before she could reach safety. "Tag, you're it!" Jodi yelled.

The girls played their game for several more rounds with the three girls on the slowest horses – Tessa, Jodi, and Claire – the ones to be tagged. Andi and Gina consistently outran the tagged person in their sprint back to home base.

When the game ended, the girls led their horses over to the water trough. The horses drank from the metal reservoir while the girls took turns sipping from the water hose and hosing off their horses. The cool water was a welcome reprieve after hiding and sprinting in the hot summer afternoon. Then the group retreated to the shade of a large live oak.

Jodi turned to Gina. "Tessa said you saved your money for two years until you had enough to buy Buck. Is that right?"

"Yep, I sure did," Gina replied. "When I was 11-years-old, my mom took me to a farm to ride a horse. That day, I fell in love with horses and knew I had to have one of my own." Unbeknownst to Gina or to her parents, that outing was the beginning of a horse love affair that would enamor this cowgirl for the rest of her teenage years.

Gina continued her story. "I kept asking my parents to buy me a horse, but they said no, we couldn't afford it. So, I asked them if I saved up my money to buy a horse, could I have one. They agreed, figuring no 11-year-old could save enough money to buy a horse."

"How did you earn the money?" Jodi asked.

"My daddy had an old push lawn mower so I asked my neighbors if they would pay me to mow their lawns. I charged them whatever they were willin' to pay. Some paid me $2 dollars, some paid me $5 dollars, one person even gave me $10 dollars. After that first summer, I had saved over $40 dollars, but I figured that wasn't enough to find a good horse." She smiled at Jodi and chuckled. "There ain't many horses around here you can buy for $15 dollars."

Jodi wanted to hear more of the story. "What did you do then?"

One of my neighbors owns a gas station on Williston Road, so I asked him if I could work for him and pump gas. I was 12 by then, but since I am tall for my age, he didn't realize I was so young. I mowed lawns in the mornings and rode my bike to the gas station in the afternoon to pump gas and earn more money. When I had $145 dollars, I announced to my parents that I finally had enough money to buy a horse."

"What did they say then?" Jodi asked.

"They couldn't say no. With the money rolled up in a big wad and stuffed inside a glass jar, my dad drove me over to see this 2-year-old bay gelding that was advertised for sale in the newspaper." Gina reached over and petted Buck on the neck. "He wasn't trained, but when I tried him out, he didn't try to buck me off or run away with me. I told my dad he's the horse I want, so we bought him with the money I had saved."

Claire entered the conversation. "Why did you name him Buck if he didn't try to buck you off?"

"Oh, that's a good one. When we brought him home, my brother wanted to ride him too. He threw a fit saying he could ride a horse as good as me. Well, Buck didn't think so, and he just bucked him right off." Gina laughed as she recounted the story. "After that, the name stuck."

Andi looked over at Gina. "Tell Jodi about the tack."

"My parents didn't have money to buy me a saddle, so I had to ride him bareback. At first, I didn't care, I was so happy to

## Chapter 20

finally have a horse. My daddy did buy me a bridle though. He found one for $9 dollars at the feed store."

Tessa added to the story. "You finally got a bareback pad, so you didn't have to ride bareback all the time."

"Yeah," Gina nodded. "His withers stuck up so much that I got tired of riding on his boney back. I needed some padding, so I started mowing yards again and saved up enough money to buy a bareback pad."

"The bareback pad didn't help you stay on Buck any better, did it," Andi joked.

"No, it didn't," Gina replied. "I fell off Buck so many times, especially during the first few months when I was learning to ride." Gina shot Andi a playful scowl. "Or when you pulled your little pranks on me and made me fall off."

"I don't remember pulling any pranks on you." Andi countered innocently.

"How about when you threw pine cones at me or dodged spider webs in the trail at the last minute so I would run into them? Those kinds of pranks sometimes made me fall off Buck. And you're still pulling your pranks, like today when you slung me forward on my bike."

Andi laughed as she looked over at the other girls. "When we cantered down the dirt road no one rode behind Gina 'cause we didn't want to step on her when she fell off. So, we made her go last."

"I would fall off in slow motion and slide down Buck's neck. Lucky for me, Buck would stop and patiently wait for me to climb back on him. Then we'd canter fast to catch up with the others."

Kris interjected. "Yeah, Gina's right, Andi's full of pranks. But Gina, you're not above pulling pranks yourself. Remember just a few weeks ago, when you and Andi lifted me off Patches when we were cantering down Power Line Road?"

"Really?" Claire exclaimed. "I sure wish I'd seen that."

Andi continued to needle her friend. "We can do it again."

"Oh no," Kris countered. "Not again. It's no fun cantering in midair."

The other girls laughed. They all knew Andi was the jokester in the group, and they had to admit that many of her pranks were pretty darn clever.

## Chapter 21

After a full day of riding adventures, including their game of hide-and-go-seek, the girls disbanded and headed home. Claire accompanied Tessa to her house to spend the night and to prepare for their ride the next day to Terwilliger Pond.

Claire telephoned her friends to confirm their plans and then relayed the arrangement back to Tessa. "We'll meet Greta and Patrice along 20$^{th}$ Avenue around ten o'clock tomorrow morning. Greta said 20$^{th}$ Avenue is a lime rock road just past Archer Road. It shouldn't be hard to find. We can spend two nights at Greta's house and keep our horses at the Oaks Pasture with their horses."

Claire and Tessa set off the next morning across southwest Gainesville. They headed north along the grassy edge of 34$^{th}$ Street, a two-lane road that was lined with pastures and woods. They crossed Archer Road and continued north until they reached 20$^{th}$ Avenue, the site of their meeting location.

Claire wiped the beads of sweat from her forehead. "It should be cooler this early in the morning but it ain't."

"It'll be cooler once we reach the pond," Tessa said.

Not long after they turned west on 20$^{th}$ Avenue, they spotted two riders up ahead. They broke into a trot and quickly reached the advancing girls – Greta and Patrice. The four exchanged greetings and then headed west along the desolate lime rock road.

Claire glanced at the thick woods that lined both sides of their dusty route. "Looks like we're way out in the boonies."

"Yep," Greta replied. "Not too many cars out here."

"We're not too far from the university," Patrice said. "That's where my daddy works. He teaches in the math department."

The girls continued down the middle of the unpaved road until they reached a side path that angled off to the right. "There's the dirt road that leads to the pond," Greta announced. "We'll be there in no time."

The girls spent the next couple of hours swimming in Terwilliger Pond and relaxing under the large live oaks that encircled the watering hole. The horses showed the utmost tolerance as the cowgirls dove off their backs, swam under their bellies, and held their mane as the horses propelled them through the water. The girls ate their packed lunch surrounded by the serenity of the pond and forest.

As the afternoon wore on, Patrice called out to the others. "Wanna ride up to the store and get an Icee? The store's not far."

"Sure," Claire answered. "A cold Icee would taste great."

"We can gallop across the field in front of the new hospital," Greta suggested.

"You mean the new North Florida Regional Hospital?" Tessa asked. "That's where my grandma is right now. She's havin' surgery."

"Yep," Greta nodded. "We can all wave to your granny as we gallop across the field. Maybe she'll see us from her hospital window."

The girls departed Terwilliger Pond and headed north along a narrow, winding dirt road that threaded through a shady forest. To Tessa, those woods looked different - richer and more

*Chapter 21*

exotic- than the woods she was so familiar with in her Idylwild neighborhood. Interspersed among the common trees - the oaks, sweetgums, and pines - were magnolia and hickory, dogwood and redbud, and even holly and fringe trees. The shrubs growing beneath the majestic trees - wild azalea and buckeye - were equally as diverse and unfamiliar to the young cowgirl. Tessa noticed some branches shaking on a tree and spotted a gray squirrel scurrying along an arching branch. With minimal effort, the rodent sprang the short distance to an adjacent hickory tree. A tufted titmouse whistled it's even-pitched "*peter peter peter*", while a cardinal warbled, "*pichew pichew tiw tiw tiw.*"

Claire also noticed the richness of the forest. "These woods look enchanted," she remarked, as she guided her horse along the shade-covered dirt road.

"I hope they remain this way forever," Tessa said, "so we can always come back to visit them."

When the four cowgirls emerged from the woods, Patrice gestured to the school on the right. "That's Terwilliger where we went to elementary school."

"It looks just like Idylwild," Tessa said, "the school in our neighborhood."

Greta pointed across the street to the expansive field. "There's the Oaks Pasture where Patrice and I board our horses and where you'll be keeping your horses tonight."

The pasture was dotted with magnificent live oak trees whose massive branches stretched so far outward that their fingertips reached down and gently touched the grass below.

"Wow, what a huge pasture, and look at all the grass out there," Claire said admiringly.

Tessa laughed. "Ole Speedy's gonna bury his head in that tall grass and not look up for hours."

"Yep," Claire chuckled, "he's gonna think he died and galloped to horse heaven."

The girls continued their quest north along the grassy edge of the road, NW 62$^{nd}$ Boulevard as the street sign proclaimed, with the neighborhood grade school on their right and the lush, green horse pasture on their left. The girls reached Newberry Road, crossed the two-lane street, and continued northwest toward the single hospital building.

"Come on, let's run!" Claire yelled.

"Everyone wave when we are close to the building, and maybe my granny will see us from her window!" Tessa shouted.

The girls galloped their horses past the single high-rise of the recently completed North Florida Regional Hospital, and they waved and whooped and hollered as they raced across the expansive hospital lawn. Several visitors who were entering or exiting the hospital stopped to admire the carefree cowgirls. They waved back, figuring they were the intended recipients of the cowgirls' friendly gestures.

Greta pointed to a convenience store that was just past the hospital. "That's where we can buy an Icee."

The four teens sat in the cool grass behind the store savoring their frozen drinks. They were oblivious to the advancing threat that was about to transform their idyllic summer day.

## Chapter 22

The teens were blocked by a building and did not notice the darkening clouds forming in the western sky, not until a breeze funneled cool air in their direction. A distant flash of lightning and the delayed crash of thunder jolted the girls to reality.

"Oh my gosh!" Tessa cried out. "Look at that storm over there! I think it's comin' this way!"

Patrice jumped up. "Quick, let's head back to the pasture before it gets here!"

"First I gotta call my mom so she can come get us," Greta said, as she impatiently tugged at the reins.

Patrice fumbled in her pants pocket and pulled out a coin. "Here's a dime. The pay phone's over there."

The girls retraced their route southeast toward the Oaks Pasture, but they did not go far before the deluge struck. A wall of water, merciless in its assault, enveloped the girls and their mounts. Wind gusts blew the rain sideways, first from the west, from the storm's origin, and then from the east, obscuring any hope for visibility. The riders bent over their horse's withers and buried their faces in the wet fur in an unsuccessful attempt to escape the pelting raindrops. But the rain pummeled their raw skin, and their light summer attire was drenched in seconds. As abruptly as the showers began, crashing thunder quickly replaced the serenity that had dominated their carefree day.

Lightning bolts struck uncomfortably close. The intensity of the storm overwhelmed the four cowgirls.

They pressed forward, blinded by the rain and terrified by the explosive sounds of thunder that were accompanied in rapid succession with bolts of lightning. They shivered uncontrollably, shivers brought on by both the rapidly plummeting temperature and sheer fright. The squall continued its assault on the young teens as they finally reached the gate to the Oaks Pasture. The girls slid down from their mounts and stood mute and shivering while Greta fumbled through her pockets for the key to unlock the gate.

"Oh no, I can't find it," Greta cried. "I musta lost the key when I was swimming!"

Tessa tried to shout above the deafening storm. "What are we gonna do?"

"My mom'll be here soon," Greta said as she tried to regain her composure. "She has another key in the car."

"We can't just stand here waitin' to get struck by lightning," Patrice cried. "We have to get out of this storm."

Claire pointed to some lights that were emanating from a large building across the road. "Let's head over there so we can get out of the rain."

Greta objected. "No, I think we should wait here for my mom."

"I'm too scared to wait here," Patrice countered. "I'm heading to that store."

Claire followed Patrice through the attacking storm, reins in hand and horse in tow, toward the muted lights, the only objects they could vaguely discern through the blinding rain. Greta and Tessa remained behind. The storm's fury continued unabated, with rain blowing sideways from the relentless wind, and lightning strikes so close they could feel the ground vibrate.

*Chapter 22*

After a slow and terrifying trek, Patrice and Claire reached the Pic-n-Save department store. They slogged through currents of water that cascaded through the parking lot. In what seemed an eternity, the pair finally reached the overhang of the store front. Surrounded by outside displays of lawn chairs and ice coolers and other accouterments that advertised summer fun, the girls stood scared, soaked, shivering, and holding the reins of their equally drenched horses.

Moments later, a middle-aged man sporting a store uniform emerged through the sliding entrance doors. "Oh, you poor girls," he said when he saw the trembling teens. "I'll find something for you to dry off with." He disappeared into the building and soon returned with two uniforms. "Here, use these."

The girls nodded and mouthed "thank you" as they wrapped a white store smock around their shoulders. They had escaped the rain, but not the bone-chilling cold, or the fear for their two friends who were still caught in the storm.

"You must get away from that dangerous storm," the store employee insisted. He pointed at the metal rails in the parking lot. "Tie your horses up to the cart corral out there and come inside the store."

Claire's voice was barely audible as she struggled to pronounce each word. "Thank you, sir, but they might get struck by lightning if they're tied to that metal stand." Her lips quivered as she continued. "We'll just stay right here with our horses if you don't mind."

The store's employee left the two adolescents and disappeared back through the sliding doors. Several minutes later he reemerged accompanied with a second man whose name tag identified him as the store manager.

## The Idylwild Cowgirls

The man-in-charge spoke authoritatively. "You girls can't continue to stand outside and risk being struck by lightning. If you won't tie your horses to the cart corral in the parking lot, then you must bring your horses inside the store right now."

Without another word, the two men walked back through the automatic sliding front doors, followed by the two drenched cowgirls leading their compliant and sodden mounts. Once

*Chapter 22*

inside the building, the cowgirls stared at the bright lights, the shelves of merchandise, and the cluster of people who were staring back at them.

When the storm's intensity subsided, the store manager approached them. "I think it's safe for you to go outside now." The cowgirls thanked the man and led their horses back through the automatic sliding doors to the muted gray skies and soft drizzle that had now replaced the horrific storm. They sloshed through the streams of water that continued to flow across the parking lot.

"I can't believe they let us take our horses inside the store," Patrice said slowly, still shaking from the cold.

Claire managed a momentary smile. "Lucky for us the horses only left a big puddle of water inside that store and nothin' else."

## Chapter 23

The next morning the teens awoke weary and subdued from the previous day's harrowing events. They were anxious to check on the horses after their terrifying experience. Soon after breakfast, Greta's mother drove them the couple of miles back to the Oaks Pasture where they found the four horses grazing peacefully on the far side of the field. They retrieved their horses and slowly brushed them, cleaned their hooves, and checked for any signs of injury.

The four equestrians ambled east along Newberry Road to the Sugarfoot Neighborhood where Greta and Patrice lived. They navigated along the edge of the paved roads that wound through the quiet subdivision.

"Hey, let's ride over to Megan's house and jump on her trampoline," Patrice suggested.

The cowgirls drifted the three blocks south to the dead-end where Megan and her family resided. They tied their horses to the chain-link fence and took turns jumping on the trampoline.

Megan's mother came outside to check on the loud and rambunctious youngsters and was startled to see four motionless horses tied to the backyard fence, while two girls jumped up and down on the trampoline and bounced a third one who was sitting in the middle. "My, what calm horses," she exclaimed.

*Chapter 23*

"Oh, that's nothing," Patrice replied. "Not compared to the excitement we had yesterday."

The teens described their terrifying experience while Megan's mother looked at them in disbelief. "Now I see why your horses are content to just stand here tied to the fence."

The four friends headed back to the Oaks Pasture early that afternoon to avoid encountering another storm. Before departing, Greta confirmed she still had the gate key in her pocket and that her mother would drive out a short time later to retrieve the four young equestrians.

The next morning was their final ride together. The four teens groomed and tacked their horses and trekked the short distance south to Terwilliger Pond for a concluding swim together before Tessa and Claire's long journey home.

After an hour or so of horseplay in the pond, the four friends said their goodbyes and Tessa and Claire aimed south. They navigated along the narrow woods road that wound around large magnolias and hickories and other hardwood trees. They crossed over a narrow wooden bridge, and when they reached the wide lime rock road, they turned east on 20th Avenue. They followed the hot, dusty road for a long mile until it terminated at 34th Street. When they turned south, Tessa remarked, "It's a straight shot home now."

"For you, it is," Claire replied, "but I still have to cross Paynes Prairie to get home. I'm worried about this cut," she said as she lifted her arm. "Look at the red lines on it." The injury was not particularly deep, but it was puffy and swollen, and worst of all, had streaks about an inch long radiating out from the wound. "I cut it when I climbed through the barbed wire fence a couple of days ago. It musta gotten infected when we were swimmin'."

Tessa shook her head and frowned. "I've never seen streaks like that before."

"Me neither, but my mom warned me once that red lines are the sign of blood poisoning. She said if those lines reach your heart then you'll die."

Tessa glanced over at Claire, who was visibly worried, as the two girls followed the slow, back-and-forth movement of their mounts' comfortable stride. "Looks like those lines are only an inch long. It's still another foot or so to your heart," she said as she tried to ease her friend's distress.

"Yeah, well let's hurry so we can ride faster than those lines can go."

The pair cued their horses to trot as they proceeded south along the edge of 34th Street. They hastily crossed two intersections – Archer Road and Williston Road – before reaching Rocky Point Road. At Rocky Point, they waved goodbye, and Claire proceeded east toward Highway 441, the route across Paynes Prairie and to her parents' farm.

Alone, Claire sensed that those streaks of poison had crept closer to her heart. She knew she had to race home, a race which her life might depend on. When she reached the mowed right-of-way that bordered the four-lane highway, she squeezed her horse into a canter. She crouched down over the saddle and glided effortlessly with each rolling stride. She gazed right at the western horizon where the sun should have been. The round inferno had disappeared from the sky and was now replaced with tranquil hues of orange and pink and red. But the tranquility of the sky did not calm her fear of a poison that was inching closer and closer to her heart.

The young adventurer turned onto her driveway just as darkness set in. She loosened Shotsie's reins and reached down and stroked his neck. "You are absolutely the best horse in the

## Chapter 23

whole world," she whispered. "Thank you for getting me home safely after such a long ride." Shotsie cocked one ear back as he continued his fluid stride to the barn.

Claire found her family sitting down to supper as she walked into the house. Her dad smiled and greeted her. "I figured you'd smell your mom's good cookin' and come home just in time for dinner."

"You look tired, dear," her mom observed. "Did you have fun riding with your friends?"

She nodded solemnly and wrinkled her brow. "Yeah, but I'm tired, and I'm afraid my arm's infected," she said as she held up her arm for her parents to see. "Look, it has those red lines you warned me about."

Her mom examined the wound. "Yes, it sure does look infected," she concurred. "Right after dinner take a shower and wash it really good with soap and very hot water. Then I'll clean it with peroxide and doctor it with an antibiotic ointment. That should take care of it for tonight," she assured her daughter.

After the shower, Claire should have relished her mother's nurturing and the medical attention she was receiving as she stretched out on her bed, but the brave adolescent fell sound asleep before her mom could finish applying the white protective gauze to her threatening wound.

## Chapter 24

A week later, Andi phoned the other cowgirls. "Hey, there's a full moon tomorrow night. Let's camp out so we can go night riding." The young teens were enjoying their carefree summer days, and all jumped at the suggestion for more adventure, all except LeeAnne.

LeeAnne had just returned from a week-long visit to Tampa. She was not sure she wanted to join the other cowgirls or ride Snuffy ever again. Her recent ride on that pony was a disaster when she was thrown from the frightened horse and hit the ground near a threatening gator. That accident, combined with the even more traumatic loss of her beloved Daisy, made her reluctant to ride horses with the group. But she had to admit, camping out and riding by moonlight sounded like a lot of fun.

Claire rode Shotsie north across Paynes Prairie to Tessa's house and turned him out with Tessa's horses so she could help set up the campsite. The group had decided on two camping locations - Tessa, Claire, and LeeAnne would camp in the woods behind Tessa's house; and Andi, Kris, Jodi, and Gina would set their tents up in the woods near Andi's house. The cowgirls all agreed to meet at Idylwild School at 9:00 that evening.

Gina was lost in thought as she biked over to Mr. Taylors's pasture to retrieve her horse. Had it really been a year since the

## Chapter 24

group last camped out and rode by moonlight? Gina reflected on how Crown Road glowed under a full moon and the surprising visibility that allowed her and the others to see clear across the farm fields. Barefoot, Gina pedaled her undersized spider bike at a rapid pace while she clasped a bagged-up ration of horse feed under one arm and held the upright handlebars with her free hand. She ignored the stop sign at Rocky Point Road. She was in a hurry to reach the horse pasture, and besides, that road rarely sees many cars. At full speed, she hit the raised asphalt. The bike lurched, causing the chain to derail and the pedals to jam. One handed, Gina could not maintain control of her careening bicycle. As the bike crashed, Gina's bare foot scraped across the hard, unforgiving asphalt. Momentarily stunned, she laid on the road for several long minutes before she tried to move. She lifted the bike off her body and strained to stand up. Her right foot and toes and even her shin burned. Blood began to ooze from multiple abrasions where the asphalt embedded in her skin.

Pain overwhelmed Gina. She tried to compose herself and decide what to do next. Pam's house was closer than the horse pasture or her house, so she limped to her friend's house while dragging the jammed bicycle. When Pam answered the doorbell, Gina described her accident and asked if she could clean up her injured foot.

Bravely, Gina said, "I think I can still camp out tonight once I doctor my foot.

After her foot was thoroughly cleaned, bandaged, and protected with an over-sized sock, she climbed onto Pam's bicycle seat while her friend pedaled the bike. "Wait, let's try to collect some of the horse feed that I spilled when I wrecked," Gina said. "Buck will be expecting a treat when I catch him."

When they reached Mr. Taylor's pasture, Pam fetched the horse from the far side of the field while Gina leaned up against a fence post and rested her still-throbbing foot. Gina brushed her horse and tacked him up with a bridle and bareback pad. "Can you give me a leg up? I don't think I can swing up quite yet." Mounted and mobile once again, Gina thanked her friend and departed for the anticipated campout with the Idylwild Cowgirls.

Gina arrived at the campsite to find Andi, Kris, and Jodi relaxing in fold-up chairs next to two small, canvas tents. Their horses were tied to nearby trees.

"We were wonderin' if you were still comin'," Andi started to joke. She changed to a more serious tone when she noticed the strained look on her friend's face.

Kris gasped when she saw how rigid Gina posed on her horse, her leg cocked out and her foot bundled in an over-sized sock. "What happened to you?"

Gina described her mishap including the gory details about her toenails bending backward when she scraped across the pavement. "I think I'm ok now that I'm up here on my horse, but I can't walk very well, and I sure can't get on him without help. Guess I'll just stay up here a while."

Jodi walked over to Gina and stroked the bay's black velvet muzzle. She looked up at the rider sitting stoic on her horse. "I'm sorry, Gina, bike wrecks sure hurt." She paused as she recalled her crash on that otherwise fortunate day when she first met the cowgirls. "Your wreck was much worse than mine."

Andi jumped up from her chair and looked around at the others. "I have an idea. Let's pick blackberries."

Gina protested. "I can't walk around with my injured foot. How would I pick blackberries?"

*Chapter 24*

Andi widened her eyes and grinned as she marveled at her grand idea. "You can lie across your horse's back and pick berries."

"That might work if you have a tall horse who doesn't mind standing in the briars," Kris laughed, "but it won't work for Patches and me."

"Yeah," Andi joked as she looked over at Kris's diminutive pony whose head barely reached her horse's girth. "The bushes are probably taller than your pony is."

Gina nodded, "I'll give it a try. Let's go."

The four cowgirls left their campsite in the woods and rode leisurely along Crown Road to Power Line Road. They turned west and found the bushes flourishing beneath the towering high-voltage wires.

Kris slid down from her pint-sized pony and searched for the juicy fruit. "These are delicious," she announced as she popped the first berry into her mouth.

Andi nudged her long-legged mount to a thicket, and just before his nose reached the impenetrable briars, she reined him left. "Whoa," she commanded. Bingo halted parallel to the thick brambles. "Perfect," she nodded. Andi shifted her position until she was lying across her horse's back. She stretched out her long arms and began harvesting the multi-seeded fruit.

Gina mimicked Andi's prostrate position, carefully moving her body while protecting her injured foot until she too was draped across her four-legged friend.

When Andi exhausted the available fruit that was within arm's reach of her stationary horse, she reached down and gently pressed her index finger into her horse's barrel. Her compliant mount responded to the one-sided signal and hesitantly walked forward. "Whoa," Andi commanded after several steps. "Perfect," she smiled, "right in front of more berries."

The girls continued their harvest, with Kris and Jodi standing next to their horses in the more conventional berry-picking position, while Andi and Gina lay draped across their horses' backs.

Kris paused from picking berries to push up the glasses that kept sliding down her sweat-streaked face. "These are delicious, but I sure wish they were growing in the shade instead of the hot sun."

"You gotta contend with the sun and the briars if you want berries," Andi called out from her horizontal position.

"And chiggers, too," Gina added.

"Chiggers?" Jodi asked. "What's that?"

"Red bugs. They bite all around your ankles and waist, and they itch for a week," Gina explained.

Andi chuckled as she poked fun at her friends. "Gina and I won't get any chiggers cause we ain't standing next to the bushes where the bugs live, but you probably will," she sassed.

Jodi rolled her eyes. "Oh, great." But the threat of bugs didn't stop the cowgirls from picking the juicy berries.

As they were completing their harvest, a blond-haired lady rode up on a dark-colored horse with a prominent white star on his forehead. "Howdy," she greeted the girls as she halted the bay. She slowly dismounted while carefully cradling a bundle that rested against her chest. "How are the blackberries today?"

"Real sweet," Kris replied.

"And there's lots of 'em," Andi added.

The newcomer bubbled with enthusiasm. "Hi, I'm Stephanie, and this is my little boy, Aaron," she smiled as she glanced down at the wrapped infant. "We rode over to pick some berries too. Glad there's still a lot left."

## Chapter 24

"How old is Aaron?" Kris asked as she strained to catch a glimpse.

"He's only four months old," she replied. "Still real portable, but he won't be once he starts crawling and then walking." She lifted the thin sheet and cooed at the sleeping infant. "Riding in this baby carrier puts him to sleep every time."

"Here," Kris gestured as she extended her paper cup to the lady. "You've got your hands full. You can have the rest of my berries."

"Mine too," Andi offered. "Our bellies are full," she grinned as she rubbed her stomach.

Gina and Jodi joined in. "You can have our berries too."

Stephanie paused a moment before accepting the cowgirls' kind gesture. "That's mighty generous of you," she beamed. She reached around and unclipped a container from her saddle. "I'll put them in here with the others I'm going to pick. And now, thanks to you all, I'll have enough to make a cobbler for dinner tonight."

Kris swung up onto her pony and waved. "Nice to meet you, Ms. Stephanie. We're headin' back to our campsite and tonight we're riding with the stars."

## Chapter 25

By nine pm, the full moon had cast its bright light across the rural neighborhood when the cowgirls arrived on horseback at the designated meeting location - Idylwild School. There had been no afternoon summer showers so the sky was clear and the night air warm. "Let's head over to Crown Road and tell ghost stories," Kris suggested.

"Good idea," Andi agreed.

Gina turned to Claire and Jodi, the two cowgirls who had not participated in any moonlight rides. "The moss on the trees casts eerie shadows over the dirt road and makes it feel real haunted at night."

The cowgirls rode south through the back portion of the neighborhood until they reached the narrow winding path that ushered them through the woods to Crown Road. Fireflies blinked haphazardly throughout the forest.

"It's a good thing our horses know this trail so well," Kris exclaimed. "Otherwise, it'd be hard to follow in the dark, even with a full moon."

"Just stay on the trail and watch out for sinkholes opening up," Tessa cautioned. "I don't want that to happen to me again, especially at night."

They reached Crown Road a short time later. The full moon illuminated the eastern sky and bathed the dirt road with light, revealing the farms beyond. The road was stately with its

*Chapter 25*

magnificent, fern-covered branches that cast moon shadows along their route. But now their beloved dirt road was under assault, threatened with development by a single neighborhood resident.

As though she was reading the other cowgirls' minds, Jodi shuddered. "This road is just too beautiful to destroy. We've got to convince the county to protect it."

As the friends ambled down the moonlit dirt road, Kris leaned back and rested her head on her horse's rump. "Look how the moon filters through the moss. It's casting ghostly shadows across the road."

The full moon slipped behind a wall of clouds and then resurfaced to once again light up the starry night. A breeze from the west stirred the tops of the trees. When the soft wind subsided, the tranquility of the night returned.

Andi imitated Kris's horizontal position and looked up through the intricate network of branches, leaves, and hanging moss. "I think there are ghosts up there, friendly ghosts, staring down at us from the tops of those trees." The word, ghost, inspired the cowgirls to take turns telling spooky stories.

The scary tales were interrupted by a loud and inquiring, "*Who cooks for you, who cooks for you,*" followed by a series of chuckles and chatter.

Claire laughed. "That's an owl calling."

"It sounds like a bunch of cwazy monkeys," LeeAnne giggled.

The girls were mesmerized by the nocturnal sounds – the pair of owls that summoned and answered, the katydids that pulsated a gentle hum, the chorus of green tree frogs, and even the leaves overhead that rustled in response to a gentle and intermittent breeze.

Andi broke the group's silence. "Hey, I have an idea. Let's ride over to Highway 441 and trip the red light."

"What do you mean?" Jodi asked.

Andi started to explain. "Late at night when there ain't many cars on the road, the traffic light on Highway 441 stays green until a car on Williston Road pulls up to the intersection."

Kris continued the explanation. "When a car stops at the red light on Williston Road, the traffic light turns green. There must be sensors on the pavement that tell the traffic light when to change."

"Yeah," Andi continued. "If we all ride up to the intersection while the light is red, all of our weight should trip the switch to green."

"And then we walk our horses through the intersection like we're cars that were just given the green light to go," Kris announced proudly.

"Isn't that dangerous?" Jodi asked. "Couldn't we get hit by a car?"

Andi shook her head. "Nah, the light will be red when we ride up to the intersection, so there won't be any cars driving fast in our lane. When the light turns green for us, cars on the highway will have a red light and have to stop."

"Let's do it!" Tessa exclaimed. "It might take all of our horses to convince the traffic light we're a car and make it turn green."

The girls strolled east along the moonlit country road that they and most of their neighbors cherished. They turned north and continued until they reached Williston Road, encountering no cars at that late hour.

Williston Road was a two-lane thoroughfare that routed traffic around the south end of Gainesville. During the day, hundreds of cars and trucks traveled Williston Road, but late at

*Chapter 25*

night, the street was deserted. The girls watched the interchange from the dark corner of a mowed field that lay a few hundred feet southwest of the juncture as a car approached from the east.

"Look," Andi exclaimed as she pointed at the vehicle. "That car on Williston Road stopped at the red light. Then the light changed to green."

"So, we ride up to the intersection on our horses," Kris explained, "and make the light turn green."

Andi tried to sound authoritative, but her fun-loving voice won out. "We pretend we are a car and rev our horsie engines and ride right through the intersection."

LeeAnne giggled. "If any cauhs stop fuh us, can we wave to 'em?"

Kris rolled her eyes at her younger sister. "Yeah, I suppose."

After the stopped car proceeded through the intersection, the traffic light reset to red. The girls emerged from their observation spot, looked both ways, and seeing no cars approaching, directed their horses out to the roadway. Trying their best to emulate an automobile, they maintained a tight and consolidated mass and steered their horses into the eastbound lane straight toward the red light. When they reached the perpendicular white line that was etched into the pavement and pinpointed the stopping point, they signaled their horses to halt. They waited for the traffic light to transition from red to green. As they waited, they spotted headlights approaching from the north. The traffic light that had signaled them to halt switched abruptly to green. The teens giggled and then burst out laughing as they cued their horses forward. As the cowgirls proceeded through the intersection, the car from the north rolled to a stop. LeeAnne grinned and waved to the stopped car. LeeAnne's wave was contagious and incited the other cowgirls to laugh and wave. The two passengers in the car rolled down their windows and waved back to the exhilarated cowgirls.

After coasting through the intersection on their four-legged, horse-powered convertibles, the cowgirls steered their mounts over to an adjacent field. Still giddy from their success at imitating an automobile, LeeAnne exclaimed, "That was so much fun! Wet's do it again!"

The girls agreed to another joyride through the intersection but decided to wait a short while and watch the few cars that rambled by during the wee hours of the moon-lit night. Once the coast was clear, the cowgirls revved their horses and steered their equines onto the westbound lane of Williston Road. They halted when they reached the intended stopping point that was marked on the pavement. They stared at the red light that glared back at them.

Jodi began to fidget. "When's it gonna change to green?"

"I don't know," Andi answered. "Maybe the light can't detect we're here."

LeeAnne replied in a serious but squeaky tone. "Maybe the wight just knows we'uh a bunch of hohses and not a cauh."

Kris rolled her eyes at her younger sister's silly comment. "If the light knew we were a bunch of horses then surely it would turn green, or else it would risk us dropping a big pile of manure right here on its pavement while we waited." The group laughed at Kris's sarcasm.

They continued huddled together at the intersection obeying the red light as though they were an automobile. First, a brown

## Chapter 25

sedan coasted north through the intersection followed close behind by a white pickup truck. Both vehicles were unencumbered by the traffic signal. Then the traffic light acknowledged their presence and switched from red to green.

"Yeah!" the girls burst out in unison as they signaled their mounts to proceed through the intersection.

Once through the interchange, Tessa announced, "I'm ready to ride back to the campsite."

"Me too," Claire agreed.

The girls navigated south on Crown Road back to their tranquil Idylwild neighborhood. Fog was settling over the dirt road and surrounding foliage, and the thin sheet of dew radiated a coolness through the night air. When the road turned west, four of the girls departed on a side trail toward their campsite behind Andi's house. The remaining three – Tessa, LeeAnne, and Claire - continued on to Tessa's house.

"When we reach my barn and turn the horses loose in the pasture," Tessa cautioned, "we have to be real quiet. I don't want to wake up my parents, or I'll be in big trouble for staying out so late."

Once the horses were silently released into the pasture, the girls trekked the short distance through the woods to their tent. As they crawled into their sleeping bags, LeeAnne remarked, "That was one of the funniest wides I've evuh had." Neither Claire nor Tessa responded. They were already sound asleep.

## Chapter 26

The warm summer sun had advanced high above the eastern horizon when the three girls finally awoke. Still drowsy from their late-night adventure, they would have preferred to sleep a bit longer. But the thick canvas tent, which lacked any appreciable ventilation, had heated up from the morning sun.

Claire sat up and pushed the sleeping bag off her body. She yawned and stretched her arms. "I guess we oughta get up now. It's too hot to stay in this tent any longer."

"I'm stahvin'," LeeAnne squeaked as she sat up, pushed back her kinky ringlets, and looked from one friend to the other. Then she grinned at Tessa. "Can we eat bweakfast at youh house?"

"Sure," Tessa nodded. "My momma might fix us pancakes if we ask her to."

"I want to check on Shotsie first and feed him breakfast," Claire said, "and make sure he's ok after so much riding yesterday."

"Good idea," Tessa agreed, "especially since you rode him across the Prairie before our long moonlight ride last night."

LeeAnne giggled. "He's pwobably still asleep, just wike we'd be if the sun hadn't heated up owuh tent so much."

Tessa smiled as she silently welcomed the return of LeeAnne's giddiness. Maybe the dark sadness that had enveloped the youngest cowgirl was finally lifting.

*Chapter 26*

The girls rolled up their sleeping bags, disassembled and folded the tent, grabbed their pillows, and carried their gear back to Tessa's house. As they approached the pasture, they were greeted by two alert and hungry horses – Speedy and Snuffy.

Claire looked around the pasture, and not seeing her horse, called out in alarm. "Where's Shotsie? He should be here with the others." She dropped her handful of gear and turned to Tessa. "I'm going out to look for him in the back of your pasture."

LeeAnne grimaced. "I guess bweakfast'll have to wait 'til we find the missing Shotsie." She dropped the sleeping bag and pillow, pushed the persistent curls from her eyes, and skipped to catch up with Claire, who was striding off to search for her missing horse.

"I'll feed these two and catch up with you," Tessa called out.

Tessa's horse pasture was partially cleared and grassy at its southern half closest to the house, but heavily wooded throughout its northern segment. And a horse at the far side of the pasture could easily be concealed by the thick brush that had yet to be tamed into a grassy field.

Panic began to overtake Claire as she searched in vain for her missing horse. She thought of the grim possibilities. Could Shotsie have escaped from the pasture last night and be somewhere in the woods or along the highway? Or could he be tangled in the fence wire along the edge of the pasture? Or could he have colicked like Daisy did, and died during the night? She tried to replace those despairing thoughts with a voice of reason, but she was left with only unanswered questions. How could her big, gentle gelding disappear from the pasture? Horses are so herd-bound. Surely, he would have stayed close to the other two horses and not tried to escape. Claire called out for Shotsie but was only met with silence. And then, as Claire and LeeAnne rounded a corner, there in front of them stood a tall chestnut horse, ears perked forward, legs straddled over a large fallen tree, and just as happy to see the girls as they were to see him.

"Shotsie!" Claire shouted with relief. This time Shotsie responded with a loud whinny.

LeeAnne looked at the horse in disbelief. "He's stuck across a wog!"

Claire ran up to her newly discovered horse, jumped onto the log, and hugged his garnet-colored neck. "I sure am happy to see you!" she cried as she buried her face into his soft fur. Then she looked around to appraise her horse's predicament. "He looks fine to me," she announced to LeeAnne, "but judging by the two piles of manure, he must'a been standing here a long time."

Tessa found the other two girls just as they discovered Shotsie.

LeeAnne signaled to her approaching friend. "Heuh he is! He's not huwt at all, just stuck," she laughed.

Claire fastened the halter onto her immobilized horse and tugged on the lead rope, but Shotsie did not budge. Claire pulled harder and made clucking sounds, but the horse refused to move. "Someone needs to get on him and kick him while I pull on the lead, and maybe then he'll jump over the log," Claire suggested as she looked at her two friends.

"Not me," LeeAnne blurted out.

Tessa shook her head. "Best you do it."

"Ok," Claire replied. She tossed the lead rope over his withers, jumped back onto the log, and swung up on her mount's back. She gripped the lead with one hand, grabbed a handful of mane with the other, and wrapped her legs around

## Chapter 26

his barrel. She leaned forward and nudged him with her heels. Shotsie shifted forward and back, but would not jump over the log. "He needs more encouragement," Claire called out. "Tessa, can you find a stick and tap him on the rump?"

"Sure," Tessa replied dutifully.

"Don't hit him hard," Claire instructed. "Just annoy him," she grinned. Claire readied herself for a big jump. Tessa tapped Shotsie's rump, and LeeAnne clapped her hands. The gelding rocked back and forth and then leaped from a standstill over the fallen log.

"Whoa!" Claire shouted as she tried to hang on. "Whoa!"

After he had cleared the obstacle, the rescued horse tossed his head from side to side and pranced a stretch as a show of his new freedom.

"Yeah!" LeeAnne shouted as she continued to clap her hands. "We saved him! Shotsie's been saved!"

Tessa shook her head, "Poor horse. He's probably been standing there all night."

"No, not all night," LeeAnne corrected her as she again tucked an unruly curl behind her ear. "We weuh widing all night, wemembuh? We weuh puhtendin' to be cauhs."

Claire led Shotsie to the trough where he buried his muzzle in the water and slurped noisily for several long minutes. She stroked her equine partner's furry neck, sorry that her beloved horse had been stuck in such a predicament, but so relieved to find him unharmed. Then she fed him his morning ration of sweet feed, and feeling particularly grateful, added an extra half scoop to his breakfast.

## Chapter 27

Later that week just after sundown, Claire telephoned each of the Idylwild Cowgirls. "Some of our cows got loose after a tree fell and knocked down the fence," she explained. "My dad thinks they're on the Williams' property next to Paynes Prairie, and he wants Mary Kate and me to ride out there and herd 'em back. We could use some help roundin' 'em up." She asked each of her friends if they could ride over to her house the next morning and help search for the missing cows.

Tessa and Andi agreed to ride their horses south along Highway 441 and across Paynes Prairie early the next morning to help with the roundup. Jodi wanted to participate too but thought that herding cows required a bit more skill than she and Scout could manage.

"You can ride Shotsie," Claire offered.

"What will you ride?" Jodi asked.

"I'll ride Rainbow, Mr. Posey's horse."

"You mean the spirited stallion?" Jodi asked. "You said he shakes his head and isn't fun to ride."

"Yeah, well, I don't mind ridin' him this time. Then you can ride Shotsie and go with us on the roundup."

Early the next morning before work, Jodi's father drove her to Claire's house. Still in her pajamas, Claire greeted Jodi. "You're here mighty early. Tessa called and said she was just leaving. She and Andi will be here in another hour or so."

*Chapter 27*

After breakfast, Claire grabbed three carrots from the refrigerator, and she, Mary Kate, and Jodi headed to the barn to retrieve the horses. The two geldings were grazing together in the smaller pasture just behind the house, while the stallion, who could not be pastured with other horses else he might breed a mare or fight a gelding, was foraging in a larger pasture with a herd of cows.

When Claire returned from the far pasture with Rainbow, she said, "I'm tying him inside the paddock away from y'all." The separation didn't calm the stallion. He fidgeted and pawed the ground in hopes of moving closer to the other two horses.

Tessa and Andi arrived, and after they had led their horses to the water trough to drink, the posse of five equestrians gathered around as Mr. Hill explained the plan.

"Y'all ride through the woods to William's property," he drawled as he adjusted his scuffed-up cowboy hat. "I'll drive my truck over from Morgan Road and meet y'all there. Claire and Mary Kate know the way. We'll comb the woods and fields looking for the four heifers and two calves that got loose. Even though it's a big area with lots of hidin' places, it shouldn't be too hard to find 'em. They'll likely be grazin' with Williams' herd. Problem'll be separatin' 'em from the others and leadin' 'em back here."

As the rancher described the plan, all the horses except Rainbow stood quietly while the girls listened. The stallion, which was infrequently ridden and more accustomed to standing with a herd of bovines than with his own species, fidgeted, pulled on the reins, shook his head up and down, and nibbled at his lips. When Claire would not allow him to walk closer to the other horses, he pawed the ground and whinnied. Claire dismounted the unruly stallion and tried to calm him by stroking his neck. He settled slightly and became less of a distraction as they continued to listen to the plan.

When Mr. Hill finished, the cowgirls reined their horses east. As the teens traveled the farm's dirt road back to the piney woods, the stallion assumed the lead and set a brisk walking pace. Claire shifted in her saddle and called back to the others. "No one get close behind me in case Rainbow kicks!" she advised.

"Aren't you supposed to tie a ribbon in the tail of a horse that kicks to warn the other riders?" Tessa asked.

"Yeah, I suppose so," Claire yelled back. "But I didn't have a ribbon, and besides, I didn't want to stand behind him and tie something in his tail. So I've warned y'all."

When the young drovers reached the woods, they turned north and followed the path around the impenetrable forest.

"Good thing there's a cleared path along the edge of these trees," Andi observed. "I sure wouldn't want to ride through all that thick brush."

Tessa shifted in her saddle. "It's probably full of snakes," she grimaced.

As the cowgirls followed the trail, they chatted about the escaped cows they hoped to locate and the reptiles they wanted to avoid. But the teens were oblivious to the resident birds that were hidden in the surrounding aerial habitat of branches and leaves. Some of the birds were juveniles, recently fledged from the nest and learning to hunt for food, communicate with their kind, and remain concealed from the ominous threat of predators. Some of the hidden birds were year-round residents that would remain in the forests that surrounded the vast Prairie. And others - the vireos and flycatchers and colorful tanagers - only resided in the woods during the nesting months, and come

## Chapter 27

September, would wing their way south to distant wintering grounds in South and Central America.

Single file, they continued along the narrow path that skirted the edge of the pine woods. As they rounded a corner, Claire pointed to the woods beyond the fence. "That's the Williams' property. It's real pretty and remote, with lots of big trees and a couple of creeks. The pastures are so high above the Prairie, you can see all the way to Gainesville."

"Sounds like the view we had just before we rode across Paynes Prairie on the dike," Andi said.

"Yeah," Tessa nodded. "But I hope we don't see as many gators and snakes as we did on that ride."

The girls found Mr. Hill waiting for them at William's gate. The truck's tailgate was lowered, and two bales of hay rested in the back.

"Our cows are used to being fed hay from the back of Daddy's pickup. Hopefully, they'll follow the truck, thinking they're gonna get fed," Claire explained. "That'll be our chance to separate them from the herd and lead them back to our farm."

Mr. Hill dialed the correct combination on the gate's lock and opened it wide enough for the posse and truck to enter. After he and the cowgirls entered the property, he walked back and closed the gate. "I'm gonna dummy-lock it," he said as he adjusted his straw hat. "But when the cows get to walkin' this way, one of y'all needs to run over here and open it so they don't stop at the gate and scatter."

"Yes sir," Claire acknowledged.

Glancing around the property from high up on her palomino's back, Tessa asked, "Do the Williams live out here?"

"Nope," the rancher answered. "There ain't no houses or buildings out here anymore."

"Didn't they used to live out here in an old house?" Mary Kate asked her dad.

"Yep, that's right. Robert and Leone Williams lived out here back in the late 30s and early 40s. Their son, Jack, was born on the property in a small cabin on the edge of the Prairie. It didn't have any electricity or runnin' water."

"And no air conditioning either," Mary Kate added.

Curious about the property they had just entered, Claire asked, "Who lived in the shack before the Williams did?"

"Leone William's parents, the Jacksons," the rancher answered. "The Jacksons settled the land nearly a hundred years ago, and as I understand it, they bought the land for just two dollars an acre. When their daughter, Leone, married Robert Williams, Leone's parents gave the property to the newlyweds as a wedding present."

Tessa laughed. "What an awesome present."

Andi looked around at the expansive property. "This place looks huge. How many acres is it?"

"Oh, about 175 acres," Mr. Hill answered.

"Do you think the Williams will ever live out here again?" Claire asked.

"I doubt it," her dad replied. "The property's land-locked, meanin' there's no permitted easement for access. It'd be mighty expensive to obtain an easement, dig a well, run electricity out here, and build a house. Best thing would be for the State Park to buy the property since it includes such a large part of Paynes Prairie."

"Yeah, then it'd be preserved forever," Tessa offered.

"Just like Crown Road should be," Jodi added. "Preserved forever."

Mr. Hill called out from the cab of his pickup as the drovers began their search for the escaped cows. "Keep an eye out for

*Chapter 27*

snakes! In this heat, they'll likely be layin' up under the bushes," he cautioned. "There's some mighty big diamondbacks out here near the Prairie."

Claire shivered without saying a word as she recalled the monster rattler that she and Shotsie almost stepped on when crossing the Prairie not too long ago.

"Not what I wanted to hear," Tessa mumbled to no one in particular.

They initiated their search in an overgrown bahiagrass field that was interspersed with dogfennel and blackberry bushes, a sign that the field had not been mowed yet that year. They meandered north easily picking their path through the weedy pasture by following trails that were likely maintained by William's cows and the wild deer. Rainbow, the only stallion and least conditioned of the five horses, shook his head up and down and focused on the accompanying horses rather than the task at hand. Sweat dripped from his arched neck, and he refused to walk calmly.

Jodi noticed the stallion's unsettled behavior and called over to Claire. "I sure appreciate you lettin' me ride Shotsie. I know you'd enjoy your ride more if you were on your horse rather than Rainbow."

"That's OK. I'll enjoy Shotsie boy even more the next time I ride him. Plus, it's good practice for you to ride a horse that's more experienced than your horse is."

From the cab of his truck, Mr. Hill pointed to the left. "A couple of you gals ride over to those woods and see if there's any cows hidin' over yonder."

Jodi, Andi, and Mary Kate broke from the group and reined their horses to the hammock of live oaks, sweet gums, and palm trees. They ambled through the woods looking for any livestock that might be among the trees and bushes.

"No cows over here!" Andi shouted back.

The two groups merged back together and continued their search for the escaped cows. A short while later they found themselves on a bluff overlooking an expansive savannah that stretched for miles.

"Wow, look at that view!" Jodi exclaimed as she pointed north. "I can see all the way to Gainesville." They watched a long flock of white ibis glide effortlessly over the unbroken marsh.

"Yeah, and look how the ground drops off right where the Prairie starts," Andi observed.

"There aren't any cows down there on the Prairie," Mary Kate announced. "Not as far as I can see."

Claire pointed left toward the southwest. "I think we should search those woods. The cows could be hidin' in there."

The group reached another large wooded area and combed it for the missing cows. Gesturing right, Jodi exclaimed, "Look at that big oak tree with the resurrection fern growing on it and the moss hanging down from its branches. It's as lovely as the large oaks growing along Crown Road that we're trying to protect."

"That tree could be a couple hundred years old," Claire considered.

Some rustling up ahead caught the girls' attention. They halted their mounts and looked for the origin of the movement. The horses also detected the sound, and they reacted just as a white-tailed deer would. They cocked their ears forward, raised their heads and necks, and tried to determine if the movement was predatory.

"Me and Bingo's brave," Andi said confidently as she reached down and patted her horse's neck. "We'll take a look." She cued her Appaloosa to separate from the group but did not

*Chapter 27*

walk far before she called out. "It's the cows, they're over here!"

"OK," Claire replied as she turned to the others. "Let's loop around and come in from the far side. When we're behind 'em, two of us can ride in from the right side and the others from the left. Then we'll slowly bring 'em out into the clearin' so Daddy can tell us which cows are ours and which ones are Mr. Williams.

Claire signaled to her dad that they had located some cows. "Walk slowly when you come up to 'em," the rancher called back. "We don't want 'em to run and scatter."

The cowgirls circled around the edge of the open field and entered the woods where the cows were huddled together. The riders formed a haphazard line as they approached the cows.

"Keep it slow!" Claire called out to the others.

"There's too many spider webs in these woods," Mary Kate complained as she brushed the gooey threads from her face. "I liked it better in the open pasture."

"Be glad you're on a short horse, or you'd be hitting even more," Jodi joked as she straddled the long-legged, borrowed mount.

The wranglers coaxed the loafing cows from their resting place. Four heifers and two trailing calves emerged from the woods and into the pasture where Mr. Hill was waiting. "Good job!" the rancher called out. "Those are all of my missing cows, the one's we've been lookin' for!"

"I thought they'd be with William's herd!" Claire shouted back to her dad.

"I assumed they would be," he drawled. "But they musta gotten into a different pasture from the other herd. This'll be much easier not havin' to separate 'em out from the others." He started with his instructions. "I'll drive slowly toward the gate, and hopefully they'll follow my truck. Claire, you stay on their right side and Mary Kate, you get on their left. Your jobs are to keep 'em from breakin' out of the pack. The rest of you gals walk behind 'em and keep pushin' 'em forward."

The procession of bovines and equines ambled east along the upper terrace that overlooked the expansive green plain of Paynes Prairie. The riders all kept their horses slow and quiet, all except Claire and her animated stallion. As they walked toward the gate, Rainbow sensed that he was headed home. The excitement of leading a small herd of cows, combined with his barn-sour behavior, caused the stallion to become more melodramatic and unruly. He shook his head and sounded with outbursts of whinnies. He trotted and pranced and refused Claire's signals to walk. The stallion's nervous energy transferred to the small herd, which caused the two calves and then the cows to break into a playful trot. When Rainbow saw the cows' exuberance, he exploded.

The stallion slung his head up and bolted into a full gallop. "Whoa!" Claire shouted. She grabbed the saddle horn with one hand to steady herself and pulled back on the reins with the other hand. "Whoa!" Rainbow rocketed forward, unfazed by the command to halt. As she tugged at the reins, Claire felt a hard resistance at the other end where the leathers attached to the shanks of the metal bit. The feel was all wrong, not that soft, spongy feel of a horse's mouth. At full gallop, she stood up in her stirrups and glanced down at Rainbow's head. She realized that the runaway stallion had flipped the shanks of his bit up when he slung his head. No matter how hard she pulled, there was no transfer of pressure from the reins to the horse's mouth. This simple bridle equipment had malfunctioned, and the uncontrollable horse was not receiving any signals to stop.

*Chapter 27*

Claire knew she had to realign the shanks before she could command the horse to halt. While galloping on the out-of-control horse, Claire stood up in the stirrups, leaned forward, and stretched her hands down the reins as far as she could reach. She jerked on the leathers, and after several attempts, she successfully flipped the shanks of the western bit back to its functional position.

"Whoa!" she commanded as she again tugged on the reins. This time the runaway horse shifted to a slower and slower pace until he finally transitioned to a jerky and animated walk.

Winded and shaking from nerves, Claire turned around to look for the other riders. They were not in sight. She wondered if her rebellious stallion had caused the cows to panic and scatter. The small herd had been so cooperative until Rainbow suddenly exploded and bolted. She hoped that the rest of the group did not have to mop up a mess that her unruly mount had caused.

Claire spotted the gate up ahead and decided that the best way to contribute to the roundup was to wait there until the cavalry approached, and then open the gate for the herd to walk through. When she reached the gate, she halted her mount in the shade so they could momentarily escape the summer sun and still watch for the herd to arrive. Rainbow heaved back and forth as sweat dripped from his neck and flanks.

Several long minutes later, Claire spotted her dad's pickup slowly approaching. She stood in the stirrups and strained to look beyond the truck for the cows and horses that should have been following the lead vehicle. She waved to her dad, and when she finally caught his attention, he waved back and gestured to her. Claire squeezed Rainbow, but her barn-sour mount refused to leave the shade next to the gate. Claire squeezed her legs harder. Rainbow commenced to walk but evaded her cues by turning right and then left and returning to the gate. Claire tried to keep her potentially explosive mount calm and prevent another runaway, so she gently nudged him forward while blocking with the reins any attempt to turn left or right. He hesitantly edged away from the gate and toward the approaching white farm truck.

Her dad grinned and waved to her, "Glad to see you're OK. That horse took you for quite a ride!"

"I'm fine," she replied. "But he's terribly barn-sour." Claire could now see the four cowhands herding the escapees toward her. "I'm glad to see all the cows are still together. I was afraid we caused them to scatter."

"Yeah, they did break away, but Mary Kate and the others herded 'em back." Her dad gestured toward the gate. "Ride up there and open it as wide as you can."

Rainbow sped up when Claire turned him toward the gate. But this time he did not bolt and run off, and Claire refrained from making even the slightest contact with his sensitive sides. Claire realized an impending dilemma. After exiting through the gate, her dad would drive his truck straight ahead to Morgan Road, the only truck-worthy route back to the farm. But the cows and horses needed to turn sharply to the right and follow the narrow trail along the edge of the woods back to the farm. Her dad also anticipated this potential problem.

"Walk your horse along the trail," he said as he pointed to the path that the herd would follow. "We'll try and get 'em to turn and follow you back to the farm."

"OK, but I'm going to lead Rainbow and not ride him back. Otherwise, he might run off with me again," Claire said as she dismounted the spirited stallion.

Mr. Hill drove his truck through the opened gate and parked in the middle of the dirt road to block the cows from continuing

*Chapter 27*

straight. "Keep 'em comin'!" he shouted to the cowgirls as he walked around to the back of the truck. "Don't let 'em turn around and run back into the pasture!" He stood facing the cows, and as the young drovers herded the animals through the gate, he waved his arms and shooed them in Claire's direction. The calves bolted when they rounded the corner and ran excitedly toward the new leader.

Rainbow reacted to the rambunctious cows and tried to dart ahead, but Claire held the reins tight and blocked the stallion's efforts to run. She was glad she was leading the stallion rather than seated in the saddle. It was much easier to foil an attempted runaway with one's feet firmly on the ground and not resting in a pair of stirrups four feet in the air.

The four cowgirls brought up the rear as they slowly drove the cows along the trail that led back to the Hill's farm. Claire assumed the role of the pied piper as the convoy of bovines ambled behind her, followed by the four teenage drovers.

## Chapter 28

Andi grabbed some carrots from the refrigerator and was heading out the door to ride Bingo when she heard the approaching sound of motorcycles. Toby and Ben motored up her driveway, stopped near the walkway, and sat straddling their vibrating motorbikes. She did not greet the boys with a smile, but rather with a look of indifference to their unexpected visit.

Andi suspected the boys still resented her for the outcome of the race. She had not placed the log in their path, and if the obstruction had been lying across her lane, she and Bingo would have simply jumped it. No big deal for this cowgirl and her athletic mount. Even though her horse was faster than any of the other horses in the neighborhood, the motorcycles were probably faster, but fair was fair, and she had won the race. She straightened her shoulders to emphasize her towering frame, which at almost 6 feet tall, exceeded the height of either of the two boys.

Toby announced loudly so he could be heard over the idling motorcycle. "We think you should know that Mr. Sawyer, the man that lives in the run-down trailer over on 14$^{th}$ Street, has been whippin' his pony."

"Yesterday we saw him pop a bullwhip at the pony," Ben reported, "and just now when we rode by, we saw sores and dried blood on it."

## Chapter 28

Andi's aloofness toward the boys shifted to compassion for the pony and disgust for the abusive owner. She gasped and covered her mouth. "Oh, that's terrible."

Toby nodded at Andi, a sign that the tension between the motorcyclist and cowgirl had eased slightly. "Just thought you should know since you like horses so much," he said.

Ben offered an expressionless nod, their eyes meeting for a moment before the two boys revved their engines and motored off. Andi ran inside and called Kris, her solution-minded friend.

A half hour later, Andi and Kris met at the corner of 14$^{th}$ Street, just a block from Mr. Sawyer's pasture. Anxiously, they nudged their horses along the dirt road toward the home of the suspected victim. As they approached the pasture, they scanned the field through the tall weeds for the injured pony.

"There it is," Kris said as she pointed near the fence.

"It doesn't look good," Andi observed. "It's holdin' its head real low."

"Maybe we can coax it over with a carrot," Kris said as she slid off her mount and handed the reins to Andi. She called out quietly to the pony while she held out her gift.

The pony laboriously lifted its head and raised one ear. Kris snapped the carrot in half, figuring every horse knew the enticing sound of this equine treat. The pony perked up both ears.

"Come here little one and get a carrot," Kris cooed as she stretched her hand through the bushes that separated her from the sagging fence. The pony stared at the strangers for several long moments before it labored over to where the peace-offering awaited. "Here's a carrot for you," Kris gently repeated. The furry muzzle slowly reached out and touched her hand.

Andi assessed the pony's condition from her tall mount. "Those boys were right. There's fresh sores and dried blood on its hip and back. It sure looks like that mean Mr. Sawyer has whipped the pony alright."

Kris's heart quivered in her rib cage. "We've got to rescue it before he hurts it again," she announced with a sense of urgency. Let's sneak it out of the pasture tonight after dark."

"Ok, but where will we keep it?"

"We could hide it in Tessa's barn," Kris replied.

They arrived at Tessa's house a short time later and told her about the ill-treated animal and their need to remove it from its pasture.

"You mean to steal it?" Tessa asked.

"No, rescue it," Andi shot back righteously.

"And you want to hide the kidnapped pony in my barn?"

"The rescued pony," Kris clarified, "just for a few days so we can feed it and doctor it."

"And then what?" Tessa asked, still apprehensive of her friends' daring plan.

"Don't know," Andi answered. "We'll find a good home for it or figure something out."

Tessa began to soften. She knew she added a dose of caution to her friends' often brazen ideas, but she realized in this case, her strong sense of compassion for animals, especially horses, aligned spot on with her friends' decision to take the pony. "OK, but what do I tell my parents? I'm sure they'll notice it in the stall."

"Tell 'em the truth," Kris said. "Tell 'em we rescued it and you are only keepin' it here for a few days. They're kind to animals. They'll understand."

The friends formulated their plans for a nocturnal heist. They couldn't necessarily ask their parents for permission to

*Chapter 28*

sneak over to the abuser's farm and steal the pony. When the cowgirls wanted to do something that their parents likely wouldn't agree to, they handled their parents in the usual way. Andi told her parents she was meeting the others at Tessa's house to play Monopoly. And the others told their parents they would be playing Monopoly at Andi's house. That notoriously long board game would buy them many hours to execute the rescue.

That night Andi, Kris, Tessa, and Jodi gathered at the same corner where Andi and Kris had met earlier that day. But this time the cowgirls were without their horses. They brought a pony-sized halter, a lead rope, a flashlight, and more carrots. The girls typically planned their occasional nocturnal outings to coincide with a full moon so they could navigate along the illuminated trails, but tonight, they were grateful for the waning moon and the darkness that concealed their clandestine activities.

The girls tiptoed up the driveway careful not to be discovered by Mr. Sawyer or any outside dogs. When they reached the gate, Andi whispered to Tessa and Jodi, "You two wait here while Kris and I sneak into the pasture and catch the pony. When we return," she instructed, "open the gate real quiet like and let us out."

The two nodded in agreement. Andi took a deep breath and carefully unlatched the chain and opened the gate just wide enough so she and Kris could slip in. Tessa and Jodi stood guard as their two friends searched for the pony.

After several long minutes of searching through the darkness, they spotted a dark silhouette on the far side of the pasture. Kris crept over to the pony. She snapped a carrot in half and fed it one bite and then another. While the pony chewed, Andi slowly slipped the halter around the pony's nose and over its ears, careful not to scare the animal and cause it to flee. She gently stroked its neck and whispered, "We're takin' you away from this awful place. Just follow us."

Kris led the pony through the darkness to their waiting accomplices. As they approached, Tessa held the gate ajar for the pony to continue its exodus from its abusive surroundings. The group was starting down the driveway when they heard low whimpering sounds from behind a dilapidated car. Movement from behind the rear tire caught their attention.

"Look, it's a puppy," Jodi whispered excitedly. She knelt and softly gestured to the hiding pooch. "Here, puppy, come here little one," she cooed softly. The puppy crept a few steps, hesitated, and then wiggled closer. Jodi extended a hand, and the young canine rolled onto its back and wagged its tail. "Hi, little one. Have you been hurt too?" Jodi reached down and picked up the puppy. It stiffened at first and then slowly relaxed as Jodi stroked its head and back. Turning to the others, she whispered. "I can't leave this puppy here with that mean old man. I'm taking it with me."

The others didn't argue. They would have liberated all of Mr. Sawyer's animals if they could. They walked back to Tessa's house, careful not to speak above a whisper until they were far from earshot of Mr. Sawyer's trailer.

Earlier in the day, Tessa had prepared a bucket of fresh water, a small pile of hay, and a ration of grain in hopes of a successful rescue. The puppy, however, was unanticipated, and there were no provisions awaiting the young canine. "I'll take the puppy home tomorrow," Jodi announced as they reached Tessa's barn. "My parents will surely let me keep it when I tell them how mean its owner is."

"Good," Tessa acknowledged, "cause I can't keep both the pony and the puppy here."

## Chapter 28

"The whole time I was walking back carrying this puppy," Jodi said, "I was trying to think of a name for it. I'm callin' it 'Shalimar," she announced.

"Nice name," Tessa said, "but you don't know if it's a girl or boy."

"I hope it's a girl because Shalimar's a girl's name," Jodi replied.

"How did you come up with that name?" Andi asked.

"It's my grandma's favorite perfume, and she's a mighty sweet person," Jodi explained.

"The puppy begins its life in a cruel home, but now it will have a kind owner and a sweet smellin' name," Kris laughed.

"I just hope it's a female," Andi joked, "cause a male dog will be mighty embarrassed with such a girly name."

The cowgirls left the two rescued animals in the paddock overnight and met back the next morning so they could clean and examine both animals and medicate the pony's wounds.

Tessa smiled at Jodi. "It wasn't too long ago when we were cleaning and doctoring another rescued animal, a horse named Scout."

"That's right," Jodi grinned. "I'm so glad she wasn't abused like this horse."

"What a great horse she's turned out to be," Tessa said. "Now you're getting another rescued animal. Did you tell your parents about the puppy?"

"Not yet, but I will tonight."

"If they object," Andi laughed, "tell 'em that at least you didn't bring home another horse."

"Just a puppy that's named after your grandma's sweet-smellin' perfume," Kris joked.

Tessa turned to Andi, the ring-leader who had orchestrated the rescue operation. "What do you plan to do with the pony? We can't keep it here very long."

Andi shrugged, "Don't know."

"LeeAnne needs a horse," Jodi said. "Can't we give the pony to her? She would take good care of it."

"I thought of that too," Kris replied, "but we can't keep it in this neighborhood. That mean old man could have us arrested."

"That's right," Tessa agreed. "The police would accuse us of stealin' it rather than rescuin' it."

Jodi thought a moment. "Let's give it to Claire. She can keep it at her farm and train it like she's training Shotsie. She could find a good home for it."

"How will we get the pony out to her farm?" Tessa asked. "We can't just lead this stolen, er, rescued pony across the Prairie for everyone to see. Mr. Sawyer could drive by, and then we'd all be arrested for sure."

"I know," Kris announced. "I'll ask my brother to haul it over to Claire's farm in the back of his pickup truck."

"Can you haul a pony in the back of a truck?" Jodi asked.

"Sure," said Kris. "You just tie its head with two lead ropes, one to the left side of the truck and one to the right. Then it can't turn around and jump out. That's how we brought Patches home, in the back of my brother's pickup."

The newly liberated pony tolerated the girls' brushing and cleaning, petting and medicating as long it was frequently fed another carrot or a handful of grass or grain. But the pony tensed and cowered when one of the girls moved too quickly.

"Poor pony," Jodi whispered as she gently stroked its neck. "We aren't gonna hurt you. You're safe with us."

## Chapter 28

At that moment, LeeAnne pedaled up on her bike. "I want to see the new pony!" she called out. "Did you weally steal it wast night?"

Kris corrected her little sister. "We didn't steal it, we rescued it."

"Yeah," said Jodi. "We didn't want her to be abused anymore."

LeeAnne dropped her bike, and when she spotted the haggard animal, her eyes softened, and her mouth dropped. Drawn like a horse to carrots, she walked straight over to the pony and began to gently stroke its ragged coat.

Andi turned to the others and announced, "This pony needs a name."

The girls scrutinized the pony, trying to think of a name that was befitting the furry creature.

"I know," LeeAnne cried out as she continued caressing the pony. "Buckshot!"

"Buckshot?" Kris replied. "Why Buckshot?"

"Cause I bet it'll be tough and stwong and wun as fast and as stwaight as a bullet," LeeAnne replied with an uncharacteristic sense of confidence.

"I hope it isn't loud and explosive like a gunshot," Andi countered.

"Well, I'm calling it Buckshot," LeeAnne insisted as she turned back to the pony and continued stroking its neck.

Tessa called to the group as she started to the house. "I'm going to call Claire and tell her about uh, uh," she hesitated as she said the new name, "Buckshot, and see if she will take the poor pony."

LeeAnne looked up at the group again and pleaded. "Why can't I have Buckshot? I don't have a hohse anymouh. I need my own hohse weal bad."

Jodi walked over to LeeAnne and put her arm around her young friend. "You're right, LeeAnne, you need a horse, and we will all try to find you one. I promise. But you can't have this one. You could be arrested. We could all be arrested because we took it without askin'."

Tears welled up in LeeAnne's eyes. "But it's been abused. Wook at those souhs. Isn't it against the waw fuh that mean ole man to hit huh wike that?"

Kris knelt beside her sister and said in the kindest tone she could muster. "I have an idea, LeeAnne. Let's you and me go over and talk to Mr. Hall. He's a sheriff, and I know he won't arrest us if we tell him what we've done. And we'll ask him if it's ok for you to keep Buckshot."

"You mean our neighbuh, Deputy Hall?" LeeAnne asked as she wiped her eyes and unknowingly smeared pony dirt onto her tear-stained face.

"Yeah," Kris replied.

"Can we go ovuh theuh now?" LeeAnne begged.

"Sure. I don't know if he's home, but let's check."

As the two sisters departed on their bicycles, Tessa turned to the others. "I'll call Claire and ask her if she can take Buckshot. As much as I'd like to see LeeAnne get this poor pony, I don't think we can keep it in our neighborhood."

## Chapter 29

Kris and LeeAnne spotted Deputy Hall's patrol car in his driveway. They dropped their bikes in his front yard and lumbered up the porch steps to the burgundy-colored door. Kris took a deep breath as she rang the doorbell.

"What's wong, Kwis? You wook scauhed."

Kris turned to her little sister. "Yeah, I'm nervous cause I'm gettin' ready to confess to a sheriff that I stole a horse last night."

"You didn't steal Buckshot, you wescued him!" LeeAnne almost shouted at her sister.

As the door started to open, Kris motioned to LeeAnne. "Shoo, be quiet."

The man stood in the doorway, and his face warmed as he recognized his neighbors. "Hello, young ladies. Well if it ain't Miss Kris and Miss LeeAnne. Won't you come in?"

As the girls walked through the door, Kris realized that this was the closest she had ever been to a uniformed officer. She hadn't noticed when seeing him from a distance, how tall and especially how muscular he was. He appeared a foot taller and a half foot wider than her father. And his sheriff's uniform further intimidated her.

The girls stood sheepishly in the living room, shoulders bent and eyes cast down at the floor.

"My, you two don't look very happy. What can I do for you?"

"Sir, uh, uh," Kris stuttered as she tried to speak. She paused a moment, pushed up her glasses, and again attempted her message. "My little sister, here," she motioned to LeeAnne, "well her horse died a couple of weeks ago and, and, she's needin' a horse real bad."

The deputy looked down at LeeAnne. "Yes, I'm very sorry. I remember seeing you gals walking that poor horse during the night. And then the vet came out."

LeeAnne sniffed and quietly added, "Yes, and huh died."

Kris stood up straighter, took a deep breath, and summoned more confidence. "Well, sir, we found this abused pony. It was bullwhipped by the owner, and it has whelps on it and dried blood. We rescued the pony last night so it wouldn't get beaten anymore."

LeeAnne interrupted her sister and pleaded to the officer. "I want to keep the pony. I'll take weal good cawuh of it."

Mr. Hall turned to the older sister. "Does the owner know you took the pony?"

"Well, uh, no," Kris answered slowly as she nudged up her glasses. "I'm sure he knows someone took it but I don't think he knows who."

The man paused for a moment and cleared his throat. "I understand that the pony has been abused, and that is wrong. But you want me to tell you that it's ok that you took the pony without asking? Is that right?"

The girls held their heads down. The deputy waited a moment, but the girls did not answer. "Ok. Tell me who the man is and where he lives and I'll ride over and have a talk with him."

## Chapter 29

Kris locked eyes with the sheriff. "Are you gonna tell him we took the pony?"

"I'm not sure," the deputy replied. "Girls, let me tell you something. I know your heart's in the right place. But taking the pony without asking, even if it's been abused, is against the law."

LeeAnne sniffled again and quietly asked, "Awh you gonna awest us?"

"No, I am not going to arrest you. Not yet," he added as he smiled and winked at the girls.

That night Claire called Tessa back to announce that if LeeAnne couldn't keep the pony, then her parents agreed to let her have Buckshot, but only long enough for her to train it and find a home for it. "We know two girls who want a horse so Buckshot may work out for one of them," Claire said. "But I sure wish LeeAnne could have the pony instead."

"Yeah," Tessa agreed, "we would all like LeeAnne to have the pony, but we just can't keep it in this neighborhood, not since we took it without askin'. I'll call the others and let them know you'll take it. I'll also ask Kris if her brother will haul Buckshot out to your farm."

Two days later, Johnnie, Kris and LeeAnne's older brother, arrived in his pickup ready to transport the rescued pony across Paynes Prairie to Claire's farm. "My, my," he said as he glanced at the mistreated little horse. "That sure is a pathetic looking one. I guess it's a good thing LeeAnne can't keep it. It sure looks pitiful."

Kris spoke up in uncharacteristic defense of her younger sister. "He would clean up and look good in no time. I wish

LeeAnne could keep him. LeeAnne would be a lot happier, and the pony would be too."

Not wishing to argue with his sister, Johnnie turned to the other girls. "How are we gonna load up this thing? I don't suppose it'll jump up into the back of the truck and I sure don't think we can pick it up."

Tessa's father walked out of his workshop when he saw the visitor arrive. "Howdy," Mr. Brown said as he reached out to shake Johnnie's hand. "You can drive your truck through that gate over there and back up to that slope."

Johnnie dodged several trees as he maneuvered his truck through the horse pasture and over to the slope that would serve as a loading ramp. "I'm gonna back up some more," he called out to Kris. "Tell me when the tailgate touches the slope."

Kris shouted when he reached the spot. "Whoa, that's far enough. The slope's not high enough," she reported. "Your tailgate is about a foot higher than the slope is."

Johnnie walked back to examine the gap that separated the slope from the tailgate. "That ain't too high for the pony to step up on, is it?" he asked.

Mr. Brown walked up. "I think we should support your tailgate so it doesn't move when the pony steps on it. We don't want to damage it."

"I know," Tessa called out. "I'll put my mounting block under it. It should be just about the right height."

"While you're trying to load that pony, Johnnie and I'll go inside and have us a glass of iced tea."

Kris led Buckshot to the back of the truck while Andi carried a bucket of sweet feed. Andi stepped into the back of the pickup and began shaking the bucket. The pony perked up both ears and took a step toward the tailgate.

*Chapter 29*

"Good," Andi praised. "Have some feed," she said as she allowed Buckshot to take a single brief bite. Then she removed the bucket and backed up a step. "Here, want another bite? You'll have to walk toward me to get another bite." Buckshot took another step forward. He stretched out his neck until his lips reached the bucket. "Good boy, here's another bite."

The cowgirls continued coaxing the pony to step up onto the truck's tailgate, but he braced his front feet just a few inches shy of the truck. In his desire for more food, Buckshot stretched his neck out as far as he could, but he would not take another step toward the truck.

"I have an idea," Kris said as she handed her friend the cotton lead. "Andi, you take the lead rope and keep his head pointed toward you and the bucket. Tessa, let's you and me lock arms, and next time he stretches his neck toward the feed, we'll push him into the truck. We have to time it, so we push when he's leanin' forward."

Tessa and Kris slipped back to the pony's rear while Andi maintained the pony's interest by shaking the feed bucket. Buckshot cocked his ears forward, and when he reached for another bite, Kris and Tessa locked hands and shoved the horse. Buckshot leaped into the back of the truck, almost knocking Andi over in the process.

"Quick, close the tailgate!" Tessa shouted.

Kris handed Andi a second lead rope. "Clip this lead to his halter and we'll tie the ropes to both sides of the truck."

Mr. Brown and Johnnie heard the commotion and soon joined the girls in the pasture. "Good job gals, good job!" Mr. Brown said as he praised the girls. Turning his attention to the driver, he said, "Now who's gonna ride with Johnnie to deliver the pony to his new home?"

*The Idylwild Cowgirls*

All three girls squeezed into the front seat with Johnnie. They all wanted to finish what they had started, to deliver the extricated pony named Buckshot to a kinder new world.

Johnnie drove down Tessa's driveway, easing through the potholes like the girls directed. As he prepared to turn onto Crown Road, a patrol car pulled into the driveway in front of him.

"Oh no," Tessa said as the sheriff blocked their exodus.

Johnnie turned to Kris. "I thought you said it was ok to take the pony."

Kris mumbled as she nudged up her glasses.

The sheriff stepped out of his patrol car and walked up to the driver. "That's Mr. Hall, our neighbor," Johnnie said as he recognized the deputy.

And then, to everyone's surprise, LeeAnne sprang from the back seat of the patrol car and skipped over to the pickup, her brown curls bouncing with every stride. "I get to keep the pony!" she shouted. "I get to keep Buckshot!"

Deputy Hall extended his hand. "Hello, Johnnie. I haven't seen you in a long time, not since you got married and moved into town." He looked at the three girls – Andi, Tessa, and especially Kris - and noticed their confusion. "Well, I can tell you all are surprised to see me."

LeeAnne could not control her excitement. "Mean Muh. Sawyah said I can keep Buckshot!"

Deputy Hall looked at LeeAnne. "Ok, ok, let me explain." He turned back to the others. "I went over to talk to Mr. Sawyer. He asked me what I was doing there, and I told him I was checking on his missing pony. He said he didn't call the police about a missing pony, so I told him that some kind young ladies had rescued it. When he said he was going to file charges against you girls for stealing it, I told him that those girls just

*Chapter 29*

might file charges against him for animal abuse. And since you all had proof that he had abused the pony, I guess I was going to have to arrest him right then and there. Long story short, I told him I wouldn't arrest him if he agreed to not file charges against you and if he gave up the pony and the few remaining animals on his farm.

"So Buckshot's mine!" LeeAnne shouted. She turned to her older sister. "Kwis, thank you fuh talking to Deputy Hall. I know it was hawd fuh you to tell him that y'all took the pony. But it's 'cause of you that I am gettin' a new hohse."

Kris reached over and hugged her younger sister.

Johnnie turned to LeeAnne. "Well littlest sis, where would you like me to deliver your new pony?"

"Take him to my house!" she cried.

## Chapter 30

Andi, Kris, and Jodi trotted along the wide grassy right-of-way of Williston Road, laughing and joking as they recounted their clever masquerade as automobiles and their success at tripping the red light on Highway 441 during the middle of the night. Summer was winding down, and there weren't many carefree summer days remaining for horse riding adventures. Andi squeezed her Appaloosa into a canter, and the other two followed.

While gliding effortlessly with each stride, Andi glanced back at the others and called out. "Let's stand up like my Aunt Agnus used to do!" Each teen attempted to rise on their horses' bouncing back, only to slip down after a stride or two. As they transitioned their horses to a walk, Andi exclaimed, "I don't know how Aunt Agnus did it. She must have been a gymnast."

"And her horse's canter must have been as smooth as glass," Kris added.

"Speaking of Aunt Agnus, do you know what she did?" Andi asked.

"No, what?" Kris answered.

"She rode her horse up Main Street to the ABC Liquor store and told a man in the parking lot that if he'd open the door for her, she'd ride her horse right up to the bar."

The two girls looked at Andi in doubt.

## Chapter 30

"No joke," Andi confirmed. "She ordered a drink, and the bartender didn't even charge her."

Jodi shook her head. "I don't know if I believe that."

"Well I believe it," Kris countered. "Your aunt was wild and crazy, and you inherited those same family genes. No wonder you're the way you are!"

The girls continued their stroll westward to nowhere in particular when Andi announced, "Hey, let's ride to the Gainesville Golf and Country Club. That's where my daddy plays golf."

"OK," Kris replied. "Do you know how to get there?"

"Yeah, I think so. We keep heading this way until we cross under the interstate. Then we turn left on some road. I'm sure I'll recognize it."

Traffic was light along Williston Road, the east/west artery that traversed the south end of Gainesville. The teens crossed 34th Street and continued west across several paved entrances that led to a gas station, hotel, and restaurant. They hoofed it under the overpass of I-75 and laughed at the sounds and vibrations of the speeding cars that zoomed overhead.

Andi pointed up ahead. "That looks like the entrance to the country club."

They entered a subdivision of upscale houses with expansive lawns. "Wow, this is a whole lot fancier than our neighborhood," Kris exclaimed.

Andi motioned to the right. "I think the golf course is behind those houses over there."

The girls crossed a narrow, paved road and cut between two houses to reach the fairway.

"There's a pond," Jodi said as she pointed to the left." Let's give the horses a drink."

The three cowgirls rode across the meticulously mowed grass, crossed a sand trap, and traversed another section of the fairway until they reached a small pond. The watering hole was a welcomed relief for the parched horses, and the shade cast by the laurel oaks and red maples that lined the pond was equally appreciated by the teens. The cowgirls savored the shade while their horses chewed on the lush and heavily fertilized turf. Grass never tasted so sweet.

After a long and lazy siesta, the trio mounted their horses and set off to explore the golf course. Kris called out to the others. "See that yellow flag pole over there? I'll race you to it."

Kris kicked her pony and Patches lumbered into a bouncy trot. She kicked several more times until she coaxed her pony into a canter. Before Jodi could signal her horse, Scout broke into a lope and followed the leader. Knowing she had the fastest horse, Andi purposely held her horse back until the front runners were within 50 feet of the yellow flag pole. Then she leaned forward, and without any signal, Bingo shot ahead and quickly overtook the two horses. As Andi passed the others, she yelled, "Let's run to that other pole over there. Follow me!"

The three girls galloped their horses across the fairway, crossing sand traps and circling flag poles like they were barrels on a barrel racing course. Chunks of sod flew through the air as the sharp hooves sliced through the tender greens. This golf course was the most unencumbered riding arena the girls had ever encountered.

The girls slowed to a bouncy trot following their exhilarating gallop.

"Oh, no!" Jodi cried out as she pointed to some men in golf carts. "I think they're chasing us and they sure look mad!"

The passenger in the front cart motioned wildly.

"What should we do?" Jodi asked.

## Chapter 30

"Let's take off running," Andi replied. "I bet they can't catch us."

"They couldn't catch you," said Kris, "cause you and Bingo could outrun those golf carts. But they would surely catch Jodi and me."

Jodi halted Scout and turned to face the approaching men. The other two responded likewise.

"What do you think you girls are doing?" shouted the driver in the first cart as he approached the riders. "You're tearing up our golf course!"

"Do you know how much damage you girls have caused?" bellowed his passenger.

"It's going to take us weeks to repair all of this damage and cost us hundreds of dollars," shrieked the other driver.

"Oh, we're so sorry," Jodi replied. "We didn't realize our horses were tearing up your golf course."

"What's your names?" the driver in the first cart growled.

Kris offered a false name while Jodi and Andi presented their correct names.

"Andrea Turner. Are you David Turner's daughter?" asked the driver in the second cart.

Andi mumbled a barely audible response. "Yes sir, I am."

## Chapter 31

Andi's father, who was an active member of the Gainesville Golf and Country Club, was notified of his daughter's and her accomplices' destructive horse racing activities across the manicured greens. Mr. Turner contacted the other parents, and consequently, all three girls were grounded from riding their horses for a week. In addition, the three cowgirls were required to work at the club each morning while they were forbidden to ride.

The parents rotated dropping the trio off early each morning and picking them up around noon when they had completed their work assignments. Their primary chore was filling in the hoof holes caused by their racing escapades. After that chore was completed, they weeded the flower gardens around the buildings, cleaned the swimming pool, washed windows at the restaurant and clubhouse, emptied garbage cans, and performed a host of other chores. Except for Daisy's death, this was the low point of their otherwise adventure-packed summer. But all three girls accepted the punishment for their destructive activities and acknowledged their poor judgment.

Jodi was particularly grateful that she had rescued and acquired Shalimar, her new puppy, before the golf course incident, because her dad's response was, "Young lady, it's a good thing you got that dog before all this happened. Otherwise, you wouldn't have kept that puppy." She vowed to not have any

## Chapter 31

more lapses of judgment. She loved both of her rescued pets, and she wanted to show her parents she was responsible enough to have them.

Late one afternoon Kris was sulking around her house. She was tired of waking up early every morning to work at the golf course. She was still grounded, and she missed riding Patches. And she hated spending the afternoons stuck indoors and knowing her sister, LeeAnne, was out enjoying her new pony. The telephone rang and Kris grumbled over whether she should even answer it. The persistent rings finally beckoned her to lift the receiver from the box that was attached to the kitchen wall.

"Hi, Kris? This is Mrs. West. I called to tell you that the county decided to designate Crown Road as an official *Scenic Road*. It will be the first Scenic Road in Alachua County."

Kris stood stone-faced as she held the receiver. "Is that good?" she asked.

"It's great!" Mrs. West exclaimed. "It will prevent the dirt road from ever being widened and paved. It also requires that a buffer of trees be protected along the edge of the dirt road. All of the old oak trees will now be protected."

Kris's mood transformed. "That means we won, doesn't it? Our favorite road will be protected, and it won't ever change. We can keep ridin' our horses on it without the threat of all those lovely trees ever bein' cut down."

"Yes, that's right. But this is even more significant. The county created the *Scenic Road* designation to protect our road, but there will be other dirt roads in the county that are equally as worthy of preservation. Not only did we protect our road, but our actions could lead to the protection of other roads in Alachua County!"

Thank you so much, Mrs. West, for calling me," Kris said as she started to hang up the receiver. "I'll tell the others the good news."

"Oh, and Kris, we could not have accomplished this without you and the other Idylwild Cowgirls. You probably don't realize it, but you girls helped convince the county that our dirt road really was worth protecting."

## Chapter 32

"Let's join 4H so we can go to horse shows," Andi said as she dangled her long legs next to her mount's spotted barrel. The cowgirls drifted lazily along Crown Road, the *County Scenic Road* that would forever remain shaded, unpaved, and preserved. The Idylwild Cowgirls' carefree summer days were fast coming to an end, and they were grasping for new ways to extend their equine adventures into the upcoming school year.

"We don't know anything about horse shows," Kris replied.

"But we know a whole lot about ridin' horses," Andi countered.

"If we compete in horse shows we would need a saddle and boots and a cowboy hat," Tessa said.

"That'd be a problem 'cause I don't own any boots or a hat, and I like ridin' with a bareback pad and not a big bulky saddle," Kris retorted.

"Well I want to run Bingo in barrel races and pole bending classes," Andi announced, "so I'm gonna join the 4H club."

Gina concurred. "Me too."

Jodi encouraged her friends. "Your horses are very fast. Bingo would likely win the barrel racing classes, and Gina, you will probably get second place."

"I want to join 4H too," Claire said, "so I can train Shotsie to be a show horse someday." She reached down and stroked her mount's garnet-colored fur, and he perked up his ears to acknowledge his rider's tenderness.

Tessa considered the logistics. "How would we get to the horse show? None of us have a trailer."

"Maybe Mr. Taylor would loan us his trailer, the one he hauls his cows in," Gina replied.

"Kris, you could get your brother to pull the trailer with his big truck," Andi suggested, not considering what a long shot it was to borrow a trailer, truck, and truck driver.

Gina laughed. "It'd be fun. Just imagine our backwoods horses becoming show horses," she boasted.

"I'll tell you what I'm gonna do," Kris announced as she sat proudly on her pinto. "I'm ridin' Patches in the Homecoming Parade this fall. My little pony, the one my daddy got me for free, might not be a show horse, but she'll be a parade horse. And I don't have to buy a pair of boots or a hat to ride in the parade."

"We'll all ride in the parade this year!" Andi bubbled. "The parade starts at the university so we can easily ride there from our houses." Andi started formulating the plans. "Yep, we'll ride up Weidemeyer Road, cross Archer Road, and ride through campus to the stadium parking lot. That's where the parade begins."

"Where does the parade end?" Jodi asked.

"Somewhere on Main Street," Andi answered. "So, we can ride our horses home after the parade is over."

"I think Scout and I could give it a try," Jodi said, finally acknowledging that her horse might be dependable enough for the parade.

"Me too," Claire added.

*Chapter 32*

"What about us?" LeeAnne asked hesitantly as she looked from rider to rider. "Do you think me and Buckshot could go in the pawade too?"

"Absolutely!" Andi fired back as she grinned at the youngest cowgirl who was perched proudly on her brand new rescued pony. "It's agreed," she announced. "ALL of the Idylwild Cowgirls will ride in the next University of Florida Homecoming Parade!"

The girls continued their lazy stroll down their protected, shade-covered dirt road as Andi, Kris, Tessa, LeeAnne, Gina, and Claire made plans for future horse riding adventures. But Jodi's thoughts were miles away. As she dangled her legs rhythmically back and forth to her horse's slow, four-beat stride, Jodi was quietly rejoicing in her most memorable summer ever. She reached down and gently stroked the soft furry neck of her rescued companion as tears of joy silently welled up in her eyes. Her dream of owning a horse finally came true. She was surrounded by her new friends, friends that unconditionally made her horse dream a reality. This was the summer when Jodi learned that special language, the language built entirely on the remarkable bond between girls and their horses. And she now had an unexpected puppy waiting for her at home, a canine companion with a sweet-smelling name that one day would follow her as she guided Scout along the network of trails and paths and roads that comprise the Idylwild Cowgirls' equine highway.

## NOTES FROM THE AUTHOR

For decades, the 2-mile stretch of U.S. Highway 441, just south of Gainesville where it crosses Paynes Prairie Preserve State Park, was a notorious death trap for animals. Between 1973 and 1977, researchers at the University of Florida documented the extraordinary number of animals - snakes, turtles, frogs, and even alligators - that were killed annually along this low-lying segment of roadway. Alarmed by the results of the study, graduate students from the University of Florida convinced the Florida Department of Transportation (FDOT) to build a structure that would protect wildlife and allow natural patterns of animal movement across the prairie wetlands. In 2000, the FDOT completed construction of an innovative Ecopassage - two 3.5-ft tall concrete walls and eight highway underpasses. The Paynes Prairie Ecopassage won the prestigious Globe Engineering Award in 2000 and has become a model for other animal diversion projects. It continues to save an unimaginable number of animals.

For many years, the state sought to purchase the 175-acre Williams tract (featured in Chapter 27), now called the Edwards Property, and merge it into the State Park's 21,000 acres of protected land. The parcel's unique and diverse habitats, it's adjacency to the Preserve, and its undeveloped condition justified the property's top listing for state acquisition. However, a lack of available funds precluded the purchase of this environmentally significant parcel until a unique opportunity presented itself.

Sweetwater Wetlands Park – a treatment wetland that cleans wastewater and storm water from Gainesville and discharges the water onto Paynes Prairie – would not be allowed to be constructed on land on the north basin of the Preserve unless a comparable replacement property could be purchased and added to the State Park. In 2011, the State of Florida and Alachua County jointly purchased the Edwards Property and placed it into public ownership as an addition to the Paynes Prairie Preserve State Park.

In the late 1970s, Alachua County formed a Scenic Road Preservation Committee and evaluated many roads for preservation. Although Ellen West's character in this book is fictionalized, she served on that committee and was involved in preserving Crown Road.

In 1980, Crown Road was adopted as an Alachua County Scenic Road due to its historical significance, tree canopy, abundance of wildflowers, and agricultural vistas. Crown Road remains just as lovely today - single-lane, unpaved, oak-lined, and shaded - as it did during those early days of the Idylwild Cowgirls.

## ABOUT THE AUTHOR

Debra began her wanderlust horse journeys at the age of 13 when her parents moved to a farm next to Paynes Prairie just south of Gainesville, Florida. Her equine highway, U.S. Highway 441, connected her to her friends 'north of the prairie' and places beyond. Horses remained an integral part of her life for more than 30 years. In 2008, she sold her final horse, Shotsie (shown in the photo below), but his memory remains as a featured character in this story.

Growing up on a farm and given free rein to explore nature, Debra developed an interest in the outdoors during her formative teenage years. Her nearly three-decade career as an environmental scientist surely originated from those early days of unrestrained exploration on and around Paynes Prairie.

(Photograph below printed in the Gainesville Sun on September 2, 1973 of the author (left) and her friend (right) riding across Paynes Prairie.)

GOING DOWN THAT LONG, LONESOME HIGHWAY
The Last Carefree Days of Summer.

## ACKNOWLEDGEMENTS

The Idylwild Cowgirls welcomed me into their clan as a young teenager many years ago. My warmest thanks to the cowgirls - Sheri Thrift Wood, Becky Brown Munden, Donni Weaver Green, Beth Cowart Eddy, Cindy Cowart Mclean, and Lisa Floyd - for allowing me to recreate many of their endeavors and mishaps into this story, and for granting me permission to feature their beloved equines.

This book would not exist without my husband and writing partner, Bob Knight, who initially planted the idea from which this story germinated, and who assisted in all stages of the book.

Three long-time equestrian friends – Ellen Grygotis, Jill Griegorieff, and Stephanie Pierce – graciously allowed me to incorporate some of their horse riding adventures under the guise of the Idylwild Cowgirls. Ellen also contributed her veterinarian knowledge, and Jill her editorial skills, for which I am grateful.

Thanks to those who read early drafts and provided thoughtful and constructive feedback – Erika and Bob Simons, Felicia Lee, Karen Knight, Elaine Robinson, Sue Cerulean, Mallory O'Connor, Sadie Parnell, Jan Atkins, and Mercedes Panqueva. I am also grateful to Elaine Robinson, Carol Ray Skipper, and Karen Porter, members of the Writers Alliance of Gainesville, for welcoming me into their writer's review pod.

Thank you also to Sharon Minor, often just an email away, for her invaluable advice.

The sincerest of thanks are extended to my parents, Mike and Martha Sue Hill, and to all the other parents of the Idylwild Cowgirls, some who are now deceased, who entrusted us with a horse, free rein, and boundless areas in which to explore. It was with the gift of a horse that we learned many important virtues – responsibility, compassion, and friendship. And despite our many ill-conceived plans and risk-taking jaunts, we always managed to gallop home safely.

## BOOK REVIEW REQUEST

I hope you have enjoyed reading *The Idylwild Cowgirls*. If you could take a moment to post a review of this book on Amazon or Good Reads, it would help tremendously to spread the word. With so many new books published each day, reviews from readers like you can largely determine the success or failure of a new book. Thank you for reading *The Idylwild Cowgirls.*

Happy trails,

Debra Segal

For more information about *The Idylwild Cowgirls,* please visit the author's website at http://www.IdylwildCowgirls.com